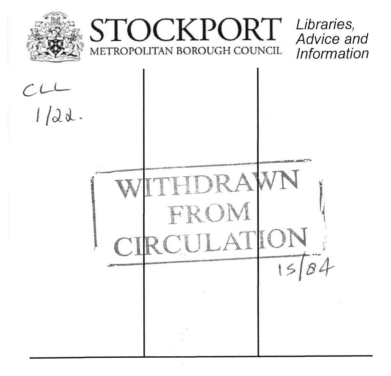

STOCKPORT
METROPOLITAN BOROUGH COUNCIL

*Libraries,
Advice and
Information*

CLL
1/22.

WITHDRAWN
FROM
CIRCULATION
15/84

Please return/renew this item by the last date
shown.
Books may also be renewed by phone or the
Internet

TEL: 0161 217 6009
www.stockport.gov.uk/libraries

Zorrie

When she reached the crest of Equemauville she saw the Honfleur lights sparkling in the night sky like a company of stars; beyond, the sea stretched dimly.

—GUSTAVE FLAUBERT, *A SIMPLE HEART*

I

out of this shadow, into this sun

Z orrie Underwood had been known throughout the county as a hard worker for more than fifty years, so it troubled her when finally the hoe started slipping from her hands, the paring knife from her fingers, the breath in shallow bursts from her lungs, and, smack dab in the middle of the day, she had to lie down. At first she carried out this previously unthinkable obligation on the worn leather of the daybed in the front room, with her jaw set, hands pressed tight against her sides, staring up at the end of a long crack that ran the length of the ceiling, or at the flecks of blue light thrown onto the legs of the dining room table by the stained-glass jay that hung in the south window. When after several minutes of this she felt her breath slowing and the blood flowing back out through her veins, she would ease herself up, shake her head, and resume whatever activity had been interrupted. Once, though, after she had slipped in the garden and landed in a tangle of rhubarb, she lay down on the daybed and fell into a deep, dreamless sleep that wasn't interrupted until, late in the evening, the cat began mewling and scratching at the side door. It took her a long time to come fully into consciousness, and as she lay there, vaguely urging her eyelids to open, aware that she was not quite awake, it seemed to her she had never felt so comfortable, so careless, so at ease. She set a feather pillow on the daybed and pulled a light wool blanket out of the upstairs closet. She began to intersperse her work in the garden and yard with regularly scheduled naps. She would lie on her side with her back to the room and look at the deep white of the wall. She would be unaware that her eyes had closed. She would sleep. Every now and again her conscience would chase her up off the daybed and back into her weedy rows or fruit-filled trees, but mostly during the time she had allotted, and sometimes past it, she just gazed at the wall or slept. One morning, well before it was time to lie down, she looked over at the pillow and blanket and soft leather and realized, with a shudder that seemed to chill and warm her both, that she was filled with longing.

SHE HAD NEVER liked to dream. After diphtheria took first her mother and then her father, she was raised by an elderly aunt who told her that people were born dreaming of devils and dark roses and should beware. This aunt, whom her dying father had only called on reluctantly, for she had drunk too deeply from the cup of bitterness after a badly failed marriage, shook and scolded Zorrie vigorously when, as happened frequently during the first months, she woke up crying. If she woke up screaming, she received a slap. Sometimes she received a slap anyway. Either because of what she was leaving behind in the dizzying hallways of her head or what she was waking to, Zorrie came to harbor what proved a lifelong distrust of the deep hours, as her aunt referred to them, when the mind played tricks on itself.

Days were different. Zorrie ran, she skipped, she won a prize at school for turning the best cartwheel. She and the other children played with hoops and balls in the yard. No one could climb a tree as quickly as she could, and there were only two boys in the school who could beat her at arm wrestling. The teacher, Mr. Thomas, would take them on long walks through the woods and across the fields. Often on these expeditions they were asked to collect interesting objects. Zorrie would run back and forth like a dog working a field, her quick hands flashing down to the ground and up again. Heart pounding, she would bring her discoveries to Mr. Thomas for inspection. He would lift each leaf or mushroom or insect close to his face or up to the light or under his magnifying glass and, with Zorrie leaning over his shoulder, or even holding the magnifying glass herself, murmur, "Yes. Very interesting. This is a good specimen, Zorrie. Well done."

When it rained, Zorrie sat at her desk and, brow furrowed, labored over her slate while the other children played checkers and spun tops and jumped around the room. She liked the musty smell of the books and the feel of chalk residue on her fingers and couldn't be convinced that the inside of the schoolhouse was meant for anything but learning. She loved the songs Mr. Thomas taught them and the stories he told about battles fought long ago. She didn't learn to read as quickly as some of the others, but when she did, she rarely made a mistake. From the start, her mind moved quickly through figures and made light work of anything to do with geography. In fact, she knew the capitals of the forty-eight states and the names of all the South American countries before several of the older children and, after whispering the names of the major European cities to herself over and over again before she fell asleep each night, received the highest marks of the school on a year-end geography exam.

If Zorrie was at home, which is where she was to be found on school days after her fifteenth birthday, she helped with the goat or the garden or the chickens or the cooking or the sewing her aunt took in. Though her ruined marriage had left her at best ambivalent about the faith of her former husband, her aunt never set aside a Lutheran's belief in the redemptive power of work, and something like a gleam, a little bit of breath on a little bit of near-burned-out coal, would enter the old woman's eye whenever Zorrie would finish a job quickly and start another one. At moments like those, her habitually pinched lips might part and a few words emerge. Sometimes it was about a plan she had once had to open a flower shop in nearby Frankfort, a nice place with peonies or lilies in the window and a chair or two on which her tired customers might sit a moment on a hot day. She would talk too about a trip she had taken before her marriage, to Bedford, where she had spent hours in a fabric store running her hands over bolt after bolt of crinoline and serge and silk. Every once in a great while her aunt would sing softly in a voice that was thin but true, songs that tended in the main toward melancholy, like the one about a man who each day put on his suit, cut a single flower from his garden, and carried it five miles along a dusty railroad track to the house of the woman he loved. Sometimes in the song he did this until the woman agreed to marry him, and others he did it until one or the other of them had died.

As their shovels scraped or their needles flew, her aunt might, on exceptionally rare occasions, offer some comment about Zorrie's parents. A blue dragonfly had once landed on her mother's finger at a church supper and made her shriek. She had loved blackberries and angel food cake and had had an uncommonly loud laugh. Her father had been good at horseshoes, bad at plowing, and given more easily than was seemly to tears. Zorrie worked, on those days when her aunt's lips parted and she spoke or sang, until her fingers ached and her eyes blurred in hopes that it might continue. She worked until it felt like there was a knife blade jabbing at the muscles around her neck. She worked until she had started making mistakes and then stopped, took a deep breath, and picked up where she had left off. Once, on one of those long days, when she had finished hemming a skirt and had reached for another, her aunt called her a good girl. Zorrie waited for years but never heard it again.

Her aunt died of a stroke three days after Zorrie's twenty-first birthday and left her nothing—not even a key to the front door—so Zorrie went to Frankfort to find work. It was 1930, and there wasn't any. She looked for a week and then walked back out into the countryside to try her luck in some of the smaller towns. One of the doors she knocked on in Jefferson turned out to belong to her old teacher, Mr. Thomas. He was balder and somewhat heavier but otherwise unchanged, and she was very happy to see him. His house was filled to the brim with books and pictures. Photographs were neatly arranged along the mantelpiece. There was a gold-framed painting of a man standing hat in hands and head-bowed in a churchyard, and a glass case of butterflies that Mr. Thomas said he'd collected over the years in fields and forests across the county. The breeze spilled in through big west-facing windows, bringing in with it the braided smells of mint, thyme, and honeysuckle. Mr. Thomas had Zorrie sit down at the kitchen table and put two fried egg sandwiches, pickled carrots, and a pitcher of iced tea in front of her. Zorrie said she liked to work for what she was offered and would be glad to help after the meal with any chore, large or small, Mr. Thomas might have on his hands, that she could sew, chop, and churn until the cows came home. As she ate and drank, as slowly as she could stand to, Mr. Thomas chewed on an unlit pipe and told her that she had been much missed in his classroom after she had left, that she had been liked and admired by her fellows and greatly appreciated by him. He spoke of her unswerving dedication to the task, no matter how tedious the lesson, and her resolute kindness to younger children who were struggling. He wondered if she had been told that he had attempted more than once, to no avail, to convince Zorrie's aunt to let her return. She said she had not.

"She was most impressive in her way, was your aunt," he said. "I heard of course about her demise. Please accept my condolences. I expect it's hard carrying on there at home without her."

Zorrie nodded and smiled. She did not like to lie even halfway to her old teacher about her circumstances, but felt too shy to worry him about where she was now sleeping, so changed the subject and asked what, now that she had eaten at his table, he had for her to help him with. After remarking that everything was under control, especially since the school year would soon be over and he could look to shoring up the home front, Mr. Thomas responded to her insistence by vanishing for several minutes and then coming back with a few pressed shirts that were missing buttons. He had a sewing kit she could use, and "spares" that matched the missing buttons so perfectly that it was clear to her that he had gone into his bedroom and carefully torn them off. Zorrie found it curious that in such quick succession first she and then he had jostled the truth for fear of incurring discomfort or upset. For a moment, as if the years had been set aside and they were back in his classroom, she had an urge to raise her hand and ask Mr. Thomas if truth was hard and impervious or soft and easily bruised, but instead she reached for the sewing kit and let the small smile that formed on her lips at the thought of raising her hand after all this time serve in place of what might have been an interesting answer.

While she worked, with the fine, clean fragrance of the shirts wafting up around her, Mr. Thomas chewed on his pipe and showed her an album of pressed leaves and flowers on one of the pages of which a pretty red maple leaf, rimmed emerald around its edges, sat between a purple chrysanthemum and a cluster of burnt-orange mycena above the neatly printed words "Specimens Collected by Zorrie Callisher on October the 19th, 1923."

"It was that day along Sugar Creek at the back of the Freeman farm. We had to go back early because of a storm," Zorrie said.

"We had to double-time it, didn't we?"

"And we still got soaked."

"It took my shoes about a week to dry. I'm not sure they ever quite recovered."

Zorrie touched at the album page, ran her finger around the edge of the mycena. "I didn't know you kept these things."

"I kept them all. Everything that could be pressed, anyway. I have more of these albums over at school."

Zorrie tapped gently at the maple stem. She had stopped to pick it up as the first fat drops of rain had begun to fall. She had not thought about that day in years but now remembered with pleasing clarity the sound of laughter and hollering as the rain started hitting them, the way their feet had pounded down the lane like they were horses in a great race, and the giant grin that had taken up lengthy residence on Mr. Thomas's face when they made it back to the classroom.

"You can take that page with you if you want it," he said when she had finished the last shirt.

Zorrie thought about it, imagined what would happen to it out under the stars where she had spent the last few nights, let alone the next time it poured, and said, "I think I'd rather it stayed in here with all the others."

Mr. Thomas handed her a sack full of plums at the door, but Zorrie wouldn't take the dollar he tried to press into her hand along with it. The meal, the plums, and the chance to think a minute about happy times had been all the wages for doing nigh on nothing that she required.

"It wasn't nigh on nothing having you here, Zorrie," he said. "Both me and my shirts are the better for it. You need anything from your old teacher in the days to come, you shout. Now go on."

She ate a plum each day for a week, then drifted west. There were others living like her—indoors when they were lucky and out when they weren't. Sometimes she would stop and exchange a word or a scrap of food, or share a stretch of road, but mostly she kept on alone. In Lafayette a man with some hump to his back gave her three dimes and a melon for helping him shift a shed full of seed bags. In Attica a woman served her a slice of ham and a piece of bread with some buttermilk to dip it in for watching her baby and darning a basketful of socks. The woman asked Zorrie as she chewed her ham if she didn't have any place or people she could go to, and though her mind flashed briefly to Mr. Thomas, Zorrie raised her eyebrows and shrugged. "Well," said the woman, considering her appraisingly and offering her a second half-slice of ham, "you're no giant, but you look like you can take care of yourself."

She got a ride on a seed-delivery truck to Morocco but thought the prospects there looked so dim that when the driver told her she could continue on with him into Illinois as long as she helped him unload his cargo along the way, she readily agreed. When the truck broke down outside Kankakee and the driver thought the time might pass more quickly if he put his hand on her leg, Zorrie struck out at him so hard he fell back, stunned, and then she ran off through a mustard field and into a beech grove. There she cried amid the pretty trees for a time about where the deaths first of her parents and then of her awful old aunt had brought her. Soon, though, she became furious with herself for carrying on and for thinking of her poor dead aunt as awful, even if on balance she so clearly had been, so she set her chin and marched into town, telling herself as she went that she had to live up to the Attica woman's observation. She asked in the drugstore who needed her to do something because she wasn't ready to starve, then asked the same question and made the same statement in the bakery and at the lunch counter. No one needed her to do anything, nor seemed inclined to rip buttons off their shirts to help her in her plight, but a kindly man wearing outsize overalls standing by the filling station gave her part of his sandwich and told her that if her eyes were good and her fingers could move fast, they were always hiring this time of year up the road a ways in Ottawa.

It took her two days to get there. The first day she walked because she didn't like the look of the drivers of the few vehicles that went by. On the second day she had three rides that took her fewer than ten miles each and then a fourth, in the early evening, that drove her right up to the Radium Dial Company's doors. The office was closed but there was a sign on the window that read "Hardworking Girls Wanted." She was standing under it first thing the next day.

She was to sit in a large, airy room in the converted high school and paint the numbers on clock faces with luminous paint. This was, she was told, important work. Not just households across the region but the mighty armed forces of the nation were depending on it being done well. She received twenty minutes of instruction, which included several comments about the safety of the dull yellow powder she was supposed to dip her wet brush into before placing it between her lips to point the tip. The powder tasted like metal mixed with the late roots her aunt had always insisted they boil and eat, even when there were other options in the pantry cupboard, and her first few attempts at making lines and numbers on the practice faces were a mess. She soon saw how it could be done, though, and her instructor nodded, patted her once on the shoulder, and told her she could now work on the real thing.

When the instructor was gone, the girls on either side of Zorrie rose as one from their places, took her by her elbows, and led her into the adjoining, windowless lavatory, where with some ceremony they had her stand in front of the mirror over the sink before flipping the lights off. First Zorrie saw that her lips were alive with yellow, and then that her fingertips were covered in glowing splotches. The girls behind her were glowing too. One of them had painted a heart on her cheek. The other had painted an eye on her forehead. Their hair and dresses shimmered. Their lips and teeth too were golden. They waved their arms and shook their shoulders and, as they giggled, sent off little clouds of glowing powder to drift through the dark.

"I'm Marie Martins," said the one with the heart. "And I'm Janie Clemmons," said the one with the eye. Zorrie's head felt like it might float off her shoulders when she came out of the bathroom behind them, and her feet felt just as light. She thought she might rise entire from the floor to twist and float against the ceiling beams. Marie and Janie shared their lunches with her. They ate at their places and had a bowl of peppermints they encouraged Zorrie to help herself to. All the girls kept candy near them to counter the taste of the paint. They laughed a great deal and made their brushes fly over the clock faces and almost never stopped talking as they worked.

Zorrie had slept the night before in the hayloft of an abandoned barn behind a wheat field that ran green and sloping in its new growth down to the banks of the Illinois, and when the day had gone to its grave, she started off for it. Janie called her back, though. She said Zorrie wasn't going to sleep in any barn. Zorrie asked how Janie knew where she was heading, and Janie laughed and said Ottawa was just a little bitty town. For her part, she planned to move to Chicago as soon as she had tucked enough away, she told Zorrie as they went back to her house. She would live in her own apartment and take the L each day and never come back home to Ottawa. Well, except maybe sometimes on holidays. She didn't like Christmas much, but Easter and the Fourth of July were fun. Zorrie asked her what the L was. Janie laughed again and hooked her arm through Zorrie's. When they got to her house, Janie hugged and kissed and shoved her way through a horde of younger brothers and sisters, and, once they were in the small room she got to herself because she had started bringing in money, showed Zorrie a picture postcard of an elevated rail line that ran thirty feet off the ground. "You'll think about clock faces tonight, but stay here a while and you'll be thinking about trains that can drop you off in the stars."

Zorrie was too tired to think about clocks or anything else that first night and the ones that followed, and was happy for it, but she never grew tired of listening to Janie talk about Chicago. Sometimes Marie came over and took a seat at the huge table Janie's mother set, and when they had finished helping clean up afterward, the three of them would step out into the quiet streets. Once or twice they met up with other girls from the plant and would walk in a large glowing group through the town. Zorrie saw her first movie in their company. She ate her first ice cream sundae with them. She collected her first paycheck with Marie on one side of her and Janie on the other, and that was the way they sat together during Sunday services. They swam in both the Fox and the Illinois. They lifted their hands above their heads and kicked their heels and shook the fringes of their dresses at the boys who were always just a soft holler away, always ready to joke and dance. Zorrie talked about home and Indiana so often she didn't even know she was doing it. One of the other girls at work started referring to her as "Indiana," but the nickname didn't stick. People in town called everyone who worked with a brush at the radium plant "ghost girls." One night Zorrie and Janie painted the bed frame of her littlest sisters with circles and squares so that it would glow while they slept. They told them a story to go with the design about a magical country filled with fairies. Zorrie thought of the landscape around her aunt's house when she told her part of the story, though she didn't say this. Marie almost always kept a tin of the company's Luna powder on her, and whenever an evening out on Janie's porch grew too dull or just quiet, she would toss a glittering pinch of it up into the air and break into song: "Ghost girl, ghost girl, why'd you grow your hair so long?"

The subject of hair was a favorite one of the assistant supervisor. He thought the young women should do more than tie it back when they were bent over their brushes and dials, that they should wear it in special hats or nets for safety, but the girls all laughed this off and told him it would look too awful. The assistant supervisor was full of ideas to combat the dangers of the world. He was somewhat deaf, from a bout of fever in his childhood, and, it seemed to Zorrie, spoke more than he would have if listening had come more easily. Radium was a favorite subject. He said it was more marvelous than gold, more precious than diamonds. He said that someday great tales would be written about radium, that they were already being shaped, perhaps on this very floor. He liked to tell the girls that he put a pinch of radium in everything he drank and everything he ate. He even put radium in the bottles of Coca-Cola he got at the drugstore and drank every day with his lunch. There was dinnerware made with radium and beads made with radium that would allow a neck or wrist ornament to glow and glow. In Europe a company had woven radium with wool to keep children extra warm. "Think of it," he said to Zorrie. "I want to learn how they do it, then try it myself to see if I can get it done."

Zorrie thought of it. She had often felt cold as a child, and even on chilly mornings at church her aunt had never let her sit close enough to warm her. If she had been able to wear a layer of warm radium, perhaps she wouldn't have missed the mother she had barely known quite as much. She asked Janie what it was like to have a mother, and Janie leaned over and gave Zorrie a kiss on the top of her head and then turned her around and gave her a quick kick in her seat and told her that having a mother was those two things, and that if sometimes it was more of one than the other, it all balanced out in the end. Marie said it wasn't kisses and kicks with her mother. It was more like breeze and wind or rain and snow. "You have to shovel snow when it starts to stick," said Janie. Zorrie wasn't sure why this was funny, but when they both started laughing, she joined in.

Often as they walked through town or down along the river, Zorrie would think of Mr. Thomas, and her sharp eye would spot something worth picking up. She took to making gifts of the abandoned nests, arrowheads, monarch wings, turtle shells, and fistfuls of four-leaf clovers she would find. Marie got a river shell that seemed to glow as beautifully as Luna paint when the sun struck it, and Janie an overlarge pearl, lost some long-ago season in the back of an otherwise empty drawer in an abandoned house they explored one Sunday after church. Janie said there wasn't anything you could buy in a store that was prettier. Both wore their gifts on strings around their necks the next time they went dancing. Hands and cheeks had been painted to glow, but it was the shell and the pearl that shone the brightest. Indeed the boys that night turned into moths, crowding Janie and Marie so closely that more than once Zorrie had to help swat them away. "You are a giver of gifts and a gallant defender and we will love you forever," they said in unison, staring into her eyes during a break in the dancing. When the evening had come to its close, and the crowd had started to disperse, the three of them joined hands and went off running through the empty streets, leaping and shrieking and laughing under a giant moon.

It was times like these that Zorrie knew she would miss the most when, near the end of her second month, she gave in to the call of Indiana and climbed onto a bus and waved to her friends through the dusty window and went home. Only there was no home to go to. She had had vague thoughts, encouraged by Janie, about trying to lay some claim to her aunt's property, but the county official she worked her nerve up to speak to said that because her aunt's considerable, long-standing debts had remained unsettled at the time of her death, it had already been auctioned off.

Still, it was Indiana, it was the dirt she had bloomed up out of, it was who she was, what she felt, how she thought, what she knew. Janie had tried to convince her that the Illinois dirt was the same as the Indiana dirt and that the Illinois skies were the same as the Indiana skies, but she had failed. Zorrie sent Janie the letter she had promised and got one back at the boardinghouse where the remnants of her wages and a job rolling Bankables at the National Cigar Company in Frankfort had allowed her to take a modest room. "We Miss You! We Miss You! We Miss You!" Janie had written at the end of her account of her days and evenings, under which Marie had added, underlining the sentence twice, "It's true!"

One Saturday afternoon not long after her return, Zorrie hitched a ride to Jefferson to pay a visit to Mr. Thomas, with the idea of telling him about her adventures in Ottawa. She had kept a tin of Luna powder and the last clock face she had painted and brought them along to show him. She even thought, in her happiness at the prospect of seeing him again, that she might offer to sprinkle his beetles and butterflies with powder so that they might shine for him during the night as beautifully as they did during the day, but when she arrived at the little house, she found the front door padlocked and the windows boarded up. A neighbor working a gardening fork around a patch of delphinium said Mr. Thomas had had a letter from the county back in July that his school wouldn't be opening up this year and had decided to move away, somewhere down around Evansville, to live with one of his sisters.

"He got that letter and was gone a week later, like he'd been fired out of a shotgun," the woman said.

Zorrie picked a sprig of honeysuckle and a handful of mint from his yard to sniff at as she went and walked back to Frankfort, wondering if Mr. Thomas had taken his books and pictures and albums with him, hoping he had. In addition to sprinkling powder and showing off the neatly painted clock face, and maybe, if she had felt bold, trying to describe what it had been like to glow a minute next to other girls under the night skies of Illinois, she had had thoughts of asking if she could have that sheet of things she'd collected after all, that she would be proud now that she was a little more settled to tack them up on her wall. It had struck her that doing so might provide an opportunity to tell him that she hadn't been entirely honest during her last visit, that she hadn't been living anywhere, least of all at her aunt's place, and maybe even that she had known of his kind gesture with the buttons, though likely that would have been taking it too far.

When she was back in her room, she put the tin of powder and the clock face, along with the letter from Janie, in an oversize Bankable box she had rescued from work. Sometimes over the following weeks, when she couldn't sleep, and she could feel the weight of the deep hours settling over her, and missed her friends, and wished that Mr. Thomas hadn't moved, she would open the box and take out the face and look at its neat, glowing numbers. A little of the Luna powder had spilled out into the box when she tried to retighten its lid, so it glowed too. More than once she only put away the clock face and closed the box when the wrens that lived in the mulberry bush outside her window had begun at last to sing the world back into being and the pillowcase she had put over the cracked glass had lit up, to her considerable relief, with its own fresh luster.

II

running together, the day falls copiously

F all, then winter, came and went, and Zorrie's job with it. She worked for a time at a dry-goods store on the town square, but filling orders didn't suit her, nor did the owner's sharp tongue, so she found another job at a seed company in Rossville and in the surrounding fields, where for some years her work with a hoe, and her regular attendance at United Methodist services, was positively remarked upon. When the seed company went belly-up and the farmer she had done work for retired, she said her farewells and packed her things again.

She went east, first to Boyleston and then to Forest, where she split and stacked wood for an older couple who lived across the street from the church. While she stacked, she whistled the tune of Marie's old Ghost Girl song. It had not come to her in some time, and it pleased her to find it again. The man complimented her on her technique, but said she was letting her mouth get too moist. He had her swallow twice and then dab lightly at her lips with her tongue. He made a remark about pace and tone. He said to imagine her pursed lips were like the smooth casing of a silver flute. Under his instruction, Zorrie took a try at "Let There Be Peace on Earth" and "Shall We Gather at the River?" The old man did his own versions. When he was finished, Zorrie clapped. "We can talk about the style to it later," he told her and had her start up whistling again.

The old couple, Gus and Bessie Underwood, had a spare room with a cot and no one sleeping in it. Zorrie set her big cigar box on the windowsill and cooked and washed and milked the cow they kept in a shed at the back of their yard. She churned butter and canned ham and beans and went across the street to the church with them and sat out on their front porch as they propped up their feet in the evening and just generally pleased them both, as they liked to reiterate, to no end. When they asked her where she came from, she told them about her parents, dead long ago on the far side of Tipton County, and the years with her aunt and about her months in Ottawa and time out on the road. She made it sound as if there had been somewhat more fun to being without a roof than there had been but thought that, in the main, she had stuck respectably close to the truth. Bessie said that she herself hadn't had it any too easy at the start and asked Zorrie if it had been very hard to be alone these last years. Zorrie said she mostly hadn't minded, which was true, then added, after a pause, that being alone wasn't necessarily what she aspired to. "What *do* you aspire to?" asked Gus with a gleam in his eye that Zorrie hadn't seen before, and which took her a moment to understand. Bessie's expression was the mirror image of·

24

her husband's. Zorrie already knew that prior to their retire-
ment, they had run the family farm near Hillisburg and that
these days their son "had the reins." This son, Bessie now said,
was about the best-looking fellow Zorrie would ever see.
Gus winked and blew a little burst of air through his own
flute casing at this.

"He arrived late," said Bessie.

"Not much older than you are," said Gus.

"We've been praying someone he'd enjoy meeting might
come along."

"And now here that someone has come."

Zorrie laughed and shook her head and said she didn't
know anything about such things, which comment landed
considerably farther from the facts of the matter than had the
improvised chronicle of her life. For she had looked closely at
more than one boy in Ottawa and talked about their neat
waists or broad shoulders with Janie and Marie, and there had
been boys whose aspect pleased her out on the roads and at
work in the fields and in the shops of Rossville, some boys
she had even exchanged glances more than once with, and
she still thought about them all more often than she could
admit without blushing brightly enough to explode. So it was
not as surprising to her as it might have been that when she
went to church the following Sunday, and the son was intro-
duced, Zorrie took his hand, looked up into his green eyes,
and found she couldn't speak. Nor could she listen to the
minister's exhortations, and when he told the congregation
to open their hymn books, she found she couldn't sing.
Standing there, wondering how Harold Underwood's eyes
had made their way down her throat and stolen her voice, she
thought first not of the handsome boys of recent years but of

another, a slip of a thing, who had once come and knocked on her aunt's door and stood there even after her aunt had threatened him with a broom and bellowed at him to go away. The boy, who eventually left, had not returned, and Zorrie had not seen him again. Still, she thought of the feeling of him now as she stood in church, not singing, his features mostly faded from her mind, his blond hair shining in the remembered evening light.

She kept up her silence through dinner. Bessie insisted that her son have seconds of everything. When Bessie put a third piece of pie on his plate, he smiled a little wearily at Zorrie and shrugged. He had large white teeth. His face was flushed. Faint ovals of sweat darkened his white shirt at the shoulders, as if someone who liked him a great deal had rested her palms there. When Harold noted that there was some nice curl of light to the afternoon air and suggested the two of them take a turn, Zorrie carefully folded her napkin and stood.

They walked under enormous black oaks, beside sprawling forsythia, past gardens that needed weeding and others that didn't, across the church lawn where small girls set loose in their Sunday dresses were playing chase. Zorrie picked up a perfectly round pebble, tossed it into the air, and Harold caught it. He then tossed it back up, and she did the same. An unusually fat bee scrabbling around in a pink rose made Harold laugh and Zorrie smile. Dogs were barking about something in the distance, and a woman in an elaborate purple hat, taking tiny steps, made her gingerly way across the street from them, carrying what looked like it might be a birthday cake. Harold told her she was the first Zorrie he'd ever met and that he was embarrassed to say he wasn't even sure how to spell it. Zorrie found her voice—not stolen but hiding in a swirl of feelings that felt as strange as the complicated country names she had once memorized in Mr. Thomas's school-room—and said "H-A-R-O-L-D."

They were married at the start of summer. Zorrie wore Bessie's dress. The Lord's Prayer was read once at the beginning and once at the end of the service. Each time she felt her eyes mist for the good brave beauty of the words—"For thine is the kingdom and the power and the glory for ever and ever, amen . . ." Gus gave out a loud trill when the kissing part came. Zorrie's lips had never touched another's, and it was true, as Marie had whispered to her during a heated scene in one of the pictures they had taken in, that looking at kissing and doing it were two entirely different things.

Harold had a hundred acres of beans, oats, wheat, corn, cows, pigs, and chickens, located on a slight rise south of Hillisburg. There was a white house and a white barn and a shed for the implements. Pig hickories and chestnuts yawed this way and that. A yellow rose grew up over a persimmon stump. The house had a bachelor's scent. Zorrie spent a week cleaning and then turned her attention to the garden. There was some lettuce and chewed-up spinach and what looked like it was supposed to be a row of onions. The baby sweet corn was entirely lost to the weeds. Zorrie called Harold over, looked at the garden, and then looked at him. Harold smiled, wrapped his arm around Zorrie's waist, and said it seemed pretty grim. Zorrie smiled back and asked him to fetch her a hoe.

The evenings were all mystery. They would carry their plates out onto the screened-in front porch and eat looking out over the dusk-lit yard to the woods and fields. Fireflies drew their greenish-yellow traces through the air, cicadas screamed, and when the sky was clear, Venus showed bright through the darkening blue. Every now and again a jay that hadn't settled would swoop by, and Zorrie would imagine that it was inscribing the improbable arc of her days into the cooling air, that instead of just flying across the yard, it had flown all the way over from the Illinois beech wood in which she had once wept. Harold would talk, in a soft voice, between bites of whatever simple thing she had prepared for them. He would talk as they washed and dried and put the dishes away. He would talk and then not talk as they lay, later, for hours entire entwined.

Zorrie slept in sweet, shallow bursts. Some nights, when she woke or couldn't sleep, the walls fell away and the coming day unfurled before her. Lying there listening to the crickets, she could feel the corn against her waist and wrists, the tangled beans against her ankles. The wet dirt sucked at her shoes. The sun hit hard against the back of her head. Zorrie, Zorrie Underwood, Harold said, his soft voice winging her brand-new name out from under his hat and across the waving green toward her. She did not dream. Harold slept like a lamb. She kept the cigar box shut, and still the deep hours seemed filled with light.

On the Fourth of July there was a picnic in the schoolyard at Hillisburg. Gus and Bessie drove down from Forest with four pies and a badminton net. The school building was considerably smaller than the one Zorrie had painted dials in with Marie and Janie. She stood a moment looking at a line of windows on its west side and realized it had been a very long time since she had held a paintbrush in her hand. Bessie made a fuss over Zorrie, gave Harold a loud kiss on the cheek, and then went over to visit with some of the older women she couldn't keep caught up with, now that she and Gus had left the farm.

It was quite a gathering. Young children squealed and chased each other while older ones organized games with sacks and balls or took turns at badminton. Some of the older teenagers had paired up and stood together, teasing each other or speaking quietly, occasionally looking into each other's eyes. A big green tarp had been rigged up to provide shade. Bessie and her friends sat beneath it, fanning themselves and laughing frequently and sipping none too daintily at their lemonade. Gus was over at the badminton net giving demonstrations. When Zorrie took a turn with one of his pupils, he leaped around next to the court, swatting at a spare shuttlecock and saying, "See, see, just like that."

Harold stood in a crowd of men wearing loose-fitting cotton pants like his own. They all had cuts and scrapes on their hands and forearms and faces burned various dark shades by the sun. One of the men stood off to the side and, as the others talked, looked out over the road to the cornfield and woods beyond. Although she would never have said it aloud, Zorrie thought he was very nearly as handsome as Harold and wondered if he wasn't slightly taller. While most of the men stood with their hands on their hips or shoved casually into their pockets, he held his strangely immobile at his sides. Every now and then one or another of the men in the group would turn to him and make some remark or clap him on the shoulder. He would smile but not respond, as if he was there and not there at the same time.

After she had played Gus to an amicable draw at badminton, Zorrie helped set up the food tables. A woman named Phoebe Johnson handed her a bright blue apron and a fistful of serving spoons. Another, Ruby Summers, asked Zorrie if she could help her fetch a punch bowl and some cups from her truck. The women were as scratched-up as the men. Few of them wore lipstick. A number of them had clearly cut their dresses from the same pattern. They discussed their gardens, their social clubs, the challenges posed by the times, and made loud, self-deprecating remarks about the food they had brought so that the others could contradict them. Nobody seemed to have to know where Zorrie had come from or how she had ended up in this part of the county. She was daughter-in-law to Bessie, and that seemed good enough for them. They pointed out their men, ballparked the locations of their farms, and complimented Zorrie on the catch she had made in Harold. At this, Ruby winked at Zorrie and said she reckoned maybe the catching had been the other way around. Ruby's remark set a few of the girls hovering at the edges of the conversation to swishing around the tables and whistling. After a minute Ruby got up and started swishing, then Zorrie did too.

They ate at tables that spilled out around an old red oak that sat in the corner of the yard. There was a lengthy prayer delivered by Reverend Carter, which conjured up troubling images of divine fury in Zorrie's mind and elicited an especially hungry-sounding "Amen" from the crowd when it was finally done. Harold and Zorrie sat with the Johnsons and the Duffs. Ernest Johnson was a quiet man with a wide face, large brown eyes, and an appetite that took several trips back to the food tables to satisfy. He partook of the ham and beans and creamed corn and various casseroles with such vigor that Zorrie felt full just watching him. While he ate and Zorrie watched him and looked around at her new neighbors, their faces shining with sweat and holiday excitement, Phoebe talked quilt patterns with Helen Duff, and Ralph Duff discussed oat yields with Harold. At one point the young man Zorrie had noticed earlier stood up from the table where he had been sitting with Ruby, Ruby's husband Virgil, and Gus and Katie Roth, and walked off toward the school.

"There goes Noah," said Ernest, looking up over a dripping spoonful of beans.

"That's Ruby and Virgil's boy," said Harold to Zorrie. "He'll help us sometimes. Solid set of shoulders. Different, though."

"He hasn't had it easy lately, the poor thing," said Helen.

"Tough row to hoe," said Ralph.

No one else said anything. Zorrie put a piece of corn bread in her mouth and chewed it slowly and watched Noah Summers sit down on the steps of the school building and fold his long arms over his chest.

After everyone had finished, some of the men and boys went over to Stowe's Ice Cellar down the street and came back with watermelons in their arms. A cheer went up when the first one was split, and it wasn't long before cool watermelon juice was dripping down fingers and wrists and smiling faces all over the schoolyard. Gus got up a seed-spitting contest that drew a crowd. After the kids were done, the adults took a turn. Harold and Virgil Summers were the finalists, with Virgil edging Harold by two inches in the last round.

Zorrie went around with a tray of watermelon slices. The juice had begun to warm, and her hands felt sticky holding either side of the tray. She didn't like the looks a couple of boys gave her as they snatched slices off the tray, and she thought she heard someone make an unflattering comment about her dress. For about thirty jarring seconds she wanted nothing more than to set the tray down, rinse her hands, run home, and hide under the bed, but then she saw Harold across the lawn laughing, with his arm around Virgil's shoulder, and a moment later Bessie came up beside her, touched her arm, and said, "Oh my glory it's hot!"

Yes, that's it, Zorrie thought.

Dusk began to settle, the mosquitoes came out, and there was a good deal of swatting. Then the fireflies started up, probably some of the last of what had been an unusually long season, and the younger children ran after them with jars. Helen Duff oversaw the laying of a fire with the idea of making things festive despite the heat. There seemed to be more couples than there had been earlier. Some of them didn't yet know how to stand close and kept leaning toward and away from each other. Noah Summers seemed to have disappeared.

Zorrie and Harold sat with Ruby and Virgil, the three of them listening to Virgil talk. Zorrie had never heard anything like it. It sounded a little like Reverend Carter's prayer, only there wasn't any religion involved. There was a fair amount about Rome, more than one or two French writers mentioned, and any number of leaps off to the sides of things. When there was a pause, Zorrie said she thought she needed a dictionary to keep up, and Ruby said, "We all do."

Harold said, "Virgil used to teach school."

"Taught me," said Ruby. "Even if I wasn't worth much in the classroom."

"Ad astra per aspera," said Virgil. "She was my brightest star."

"Virgil can speak in French," said Harold.

"That's true," said Virgil, "but what I just said was in Latin."

Zorrie said she had had a good teacher for a while but had never heard French.

Virgil scrunched up his forehead and said, "Ce n'est pas toujours facile de vivre sur terre."

"What does that mean?" she asked.

"More or less the same thing as the Latin: something like 'It's an excessively long, hard road to heaven,'" Virgil said, then added with a wink at Zorrie, "which theme, if I'm not mistaken, is what every word and verse of the Good Book is dedicated to."

"Not *every* word and verse, husband," said Ruby.

"Most, then."

They smiled at each other. Zorrie liked the way they did this, the way it made them look like two halves of the same sentence. She liked the way they frequently reached for each other's hands too.

"Let's settle on 'some,'" said Ruby.

"All right, wife," said Virgil. "Let's."

Emily Owens, who had won the children's seed-spitting contest, got to light the fire when it was ready. The wood had been laid down in a crisscross pattern with plenty of bark, kindling, and balled paper. Emily touched it with a match, and orange flames began crawling this way and that. It was too warm to get close, but that didn't stop everyone's eyes from turning in its direction. Moving light reflected off the faces of her new neighbors, made them suddenly distinct again, where before the shadows had all but swallowed them. Zorrie turned to Harold and smiled, but Harold did not see her, and a moment later Noah Summers emerged from the dark. His hair was mussed and he was soaked in sweat so that his hands and face threw off more light than anyone else's, even when he was still some distance off. He's got into some Luna paint, Zorrie thought. He walked up fast and stood with his hands held stiffly at his sides, no more than a foot away from the fire. He leaned forward, his jaw set, head cocked slightly to the left, looking into the flames. Zorrie could see the muscles in his forearm quivering. Helen Duff put her hand over her mouth. Lloyd Duff took a step forward. Virgil started to stand, but at that moment Noah looked over at Virgil, shook his head, shrugged, took a step backward, pivoted, stepped between Reverend Carter and Emily Owens, and, glowing with reflected light, strode back off into the dark.

"He's always been his own brand of bacon," said Harold that night after they had taken turns soaking in a cool bath and were sitting on top of the sheets, dipping their spoons in and out of a jar of chilled raspberry preserves Zorrie had taken from the icebox. "But what he's been through lately. I just think of it, and even hot as it is, it gives me chills."

"What was the reverend saying to Virgil as we were leaving?"

"He wants Noah to talk to him."

"Will he?"

"I doubt it."

I wouldn't either, thought Zorrie, closing her eyes, then opening them and, setting the jar of preserves aside, taking Harold's arm. "When's she getting out?"

"I don't know. I don't think any of them does. She's been in before. They won't let Noah up to see her anymore. He caused quite a stir when he tried, and they say she got too worked up."

Zorrie couldn't stop seeing Noah's glow as he had come up out of the dark. She tried to picture Opal Summers, Noah's wife of no more than a few months, who less than a year before been taken back to the Logansport State Hospital for setting her own house on fire while she was in it and for refusing to leave, so that Noah had had to carry her out. She imagined Opal, lying now in a room much larger and darker than this one and twice as hot. She tried, in turn, to imagine Noah lying in a bed somewhere in the big brown house with the green roof on the farm next to theirs, his head full of smoke and a vanished wife, but began drifting so that Noah's long body blended with sliced watermelon, Emily Owens's match, Bessie's "Oh my glory!" and Ernest Johnson's dripping fork.

THE NEWTONS' FARM formed an L around their own. The Summerses' farm made another border, and there were Duffs and Dunns scattered across the ditch beyond. Zorrie was always in the field with Harold, and because everyone helped everyone else, she soon became a familiar sight on the surrounding farms. She loved the smell of the clay-rich dirt and the warm ache that sprouted up in her neck and shoulders as the hours wore on. She loved, after a long day, walking back through the tangled beans or sweet-smelling clover. She loved being teased by Gerald Dunn or Lloyd Duff or Virgil Summers when they would meet along the fencerows, and she loved even more the twinkle in their eyes when she would put her hands on her hips and tease them back. Living at her aunt's, or during the years around Frankfort and Rossville, she had not felt the tilt and whirl of the seasons the way she did on her own farm with its busy springs, summers, and falls that went by in green and brown blurs and its long, quiet winters when the weeks seemed marked only by the scratching of the chickens or the scruffling of the pigs.

They took turns reading to each other during the cold months. Zorrie liked to hear Harold read from Psalms. She would close her eyes and, caught up in the images, which had seemed terribly abstract during her childhood, imagine God himself walking alongside her, light dripping like rain from the heavenly clouds. Often Virgil lent them books. Harold's favorite of these was Herodotus. Both of them had trouble with some of the names, and it was hard to keep track of who was fighting whom, but the stories were wonderfully strange. "Imagine that," Harold said one afternoon. "Imagine going out to fight the wind with swords." When the temperature dropped and it started coming down again toward evening, Harold bowed and presented Zorrie with a small hatchet to go with the carving knife he was already holding, and they went outside giggling in their shirtsleeves to try their luck against the snow.

Friday evenings, when the roads weren't drifted, they would drive over to Forest to play cards with Gus and Bessie. Gus generally took the game too seriously and tapped his finger on the table when he got impatient or was falling behind. Bessie had a hard time concentrating and jumped up constantly to see about things in the kitchen. Zorrie had a knack and was considered the most desirable partner. Harold took a long time over his cards, laughed a good deal, and played conservatively.

When they were done, and Gus had finished either crowing or complaining about his cards, they would sit in the front room by the fire and sip hot cocoa. One evening during the third winter of their marriage, when there was a lull in the conversation, Harold started in to bragging about Zorrie. He bragged about how she had whipped the accounts into shape, had helped him make a plan for the next year's crops, could recite a number of the Psalms aloud, and cooked so well and kept the house so clean it was like living in a luxury hotel. He went on so long about things he had already bragged about many times before that Gus chuckled, Bessie said, "I bet there's other things you could brag about," and Zorrie, blushing, said, "Stop it this instant, every one of you."

At this Harold stood up, kissed Zorrie on the cheek, did a little dance by the sideboard, whacked his hand down on the dark wood, and told Gus he'd better break out the cigars.

"I knew it!" said Bessie.

"I'll get a whole bushel of cigars!" said Gus.

Zorrie smiled, looked down into her cocoa, brought it slowly up to her lips, and took a long sip.

Mornings and odd times of the day were difficult at first. Late one afternoon, Harold saw Zorrie come out of the bathroom wiping her mouth and said she'd better rest up, that he'd take on her evening chores. She spent exactly ten minutes with her feet up by the fire before she put on her boots and joined Harold in the barn. They fed the cows and pigs, put out fresh straw, and looked in on the chickens, their black eyes flashing in the half dark. Zorrie said she felt wonderful, but a moment later told Harold she had better take his arm.

It grew warmer, and Zorrie, recalling the assistant supervisor's pronouncements about the tonic effects of radium, retrieved her can of Luna powder and took to quietly spooning some of it each morning into a glass of water. Bessie paid frequent visits and insisted on cooking some of the meals. When Zorrie started to show, Mary Owens brought Emily over to see what a mother looked like. Emily looked at Zorrie's stomach, then up at Zorrie's face, then slowly reached out her hand, held it against Zorrie's apron, frowned, looked back up at Zorrie's face, then said, "How does it breathe?"

Bessie started to say something, then stopped.

Mary said, "You don't ask questions like that."

But Zorrie said, "Like a fish," then put her face up close to Emily's, opened her eyes as wide as she could, puckered her lips, put them together, and then popped them gently apart.

The next day Harold came home from a trip to the hardware store in Kempton and said, "There must have been three or four jokers making fish faces at me." That evening they found a book on angling propped against the side door with a note in it from Virgil that read, "Thought you might enjoy this . . . ," and Sunday the minister paused in the middle of his regular fire-and-brimstone, gave them a wink, and made reference to the miracle of the loaves of bread and fish. Harold took to popping his lips as he walked around the house and made a show of organizing his tackle box and making sure he had plenty of strong line on hand for the big day. Zorrie stood behind him as he arranged the lures into rows and made a joke about whether or not it would be best to cast, trawl, or just bob. When she woke one morning the next week with awful cramps and blood between her legs, the first thing she thought in her confusion was that the fish had swallowed the hook and torn its throat.

NOAH SUMMERS HELPED out around the farm that spring and summer. A pair of accidents in the field had robbed him of three of his fingers, but his hands still looked uncommonly strong, and if they bothered him, he never spoke of it. Zorrie, who was healing slowly and under doctor's orders to limit her exertions to light chores, would carry mason jars of iced tea out to them and, when Harold claimed they were too busy to come to the house and clean up for dinner or just wanted a change, carried out sandwiches that the three of them ate in the shade of the oaks beyond the ditch in the back woods. As they sat there, Harold took large bites of his sandwich, smiled infrequently, and spoke a great deal about whatever came to mind. One day he went on and on about the events in Europe. He said he thought they were getting ready to ruin every-thing all over again, even though they had done a pretty fair job of it the first time. One of the boys up at the grain elevator had read aloud some of Kipling's war poetry to the general approval of those gathered, but Harold hadn't found much in it to inspire him to want to get shot at or gassed or blown up. Noah always ate neatly, appeared to listen carefully, and frowned.

Every now and again Virgil would come out and join them at their work. He had his own opinions about Hitler and Chamberlain. He said the war would kick the United States of America out of its doldrums. He said it needed a kick. Harold said he wasn't so sure, that maybe a kick was in order, but this might not be the right kind. At this, Noah leaned forward, pulled up a handful of grass, let it fall back through his fingers, looked sideways at Harold, and said, "I reckon Virgil knows his way around how a body can be kicked. Those boots of his may not look like much, but they can wallop."

Virgil looked over at Noah, bit his lip, and then looked at his hands. "He's talking about papers I signed about his Opal. Papers I had to sign for safety's sake, even if I didn't like to.

I reckon I would have taken it like a kicking if I'd have been in his place. If he'd have been in mine, I wonder what he'd have settled on doing."

"Not that," Noah said, a fierce look Zorrie hadn't seen before sweeping over his face. "Never that."

"No," said Virgil slowly. "I suppose not."

Zorrie glanced at Harold, who shook his head. They all sat there uncomfortably. Not two minutes later, as if she had been called, Ruby came across the field in a red apron with five slices of pineapple upside-down cake and a pail of cold milk, and everyone calmed down.

That evening, over supper, Zorrie asked Harold what Virgil had meant, but Harold said he didn't know any more than she did and then stood, took his plate over to the sink, mumbled something about the pigs, and walked out the door.

Fourth of July came and went. Gus stopped by the next day to tell them about the picnic. This year there had been a baseball game, a tug-of-war, and a sack race. Bessie had taken too much sun and was laid up. He had eaten so much he was going to have to get a bigger belt. After Gus left, Harold told Zorrie they would go the next year. Zorrie didn't say anything. She had been in the middle of sharpening blades on the back steps when Gus had arrived, and now she took up the whetstone again, chose a pair of shears to see to. Harold offered to help. She said it was the easiest work in the world and added that she imagined he had chores of his own. He said this was true but didn't move. After Zorrie had taken a few slow swipes, she flicked her eyes up at him.

"We could've gone," she said.

"I know we could. We just didn't," Harold said.

"There's no shame about what happened."

"I know."

Zorrie set down the stone, ran her thumb along both blades, then picked up the stone again.

"None at all."

"I know it."

"You say you know it. I told you I was fit to go. Everyone was there."

"I know what you told me."

"You'd think it never happened before."

Harold took off his hat. He put the back of his hand on his hip and then wiped the pearled sweat off his brow with a forearm. Zorrie finished with the shears and turned to the garden knife.

"You'd think," she said as she worked the stone down one dull side and then the other, "that this was the first time in human history that something like this had occurred."

Harold put his hat back on. Zorrie set the stone down and stood. Harold looked like he had more to say, but she walked straight past him, went across the yard to the garden, and cut some lettuce. Satisfied with the knife's sharpness, she inspected the early sweet corn and hoed a few weeds. She dug shallots and pulled up a fistful of carrots that weren't yet ready to come out of the ground. There were more aphids already flinging themselves through the air than she would've liked. An old gray cat that had taken up residence in the barn that winter wove her way slowly through the peas and waving ladyfingers, brushed against Zorrie's leg, gazed up at her, and walked on. Zorrie went inside and washed the lettuce and shallots, then peeled the carrots and cut them into disks. She took two loin chops out of the icebox and set them on a plate by the sink. She was reaching for the vinegar when Harold came in, sat down at the table, sucked in his breath.

"I just thought that maybe if I'd done more of what needed doing . . . ," he said.

"Or you thought if I'd done less," said Zorrie.

Harold's green eyes were surrounded by red. They shone in the overhead light. He looked at her and nodded.

"I have thought that."

"I know."

"And I'm sorry for it, Zorrie. About as sorry as I think I've ever been."

Zorrie sat down at the table across from him, reached out, and ran the backs of her fingers across his unshaven cheek, then took his hands.

"I know that too, Harold," she said.

THE SUMMER SLIPPED by. Harold and Noah harvested the wheat, cultivated the oats and beans, clover and corn. There was a bad hailstorm late one afternoon in early August that left them standing anxiously at the window, but the crops weren't hit hard, and after they had made their inspection, Harold took Zorrie in his arms and swung her around.

Zorrie felt her strength returning and, though the doctor still wouldn't give her permission to help in the fields, went back to slopping the pigs and keeping their stalls filled with fresh straw. There was a pig she liked, a sow she'd named Mrs. Thomas in honor of her old teacher. No matter how hot it was, when the other pigs were lying sound asleep in the shadows, Mrs. Thomas would rouse herself and come over to snuffle and lick Zorrie's fingers. Zorrie made a point of bringing her the most unusually shaped turnip or prettiest squash blossom to nibble, and if she came across any black-berries in the woods, she always shared a few of the ripest ones. She liked patting Mrs. Thomas's fat pink flanks while she ate, and always stood swatting the flies away and scratching her ears a few minutes before moving on.

Mornings, after Harold had left the house, Zorrie took long walks along the ditch and through the fields to build up her endurance. On one of these walks she came out of the corn and met Noah along the fencerow that split their farms. They moved together quietly on either side of the fence for a time, and then Noah asked Zorrie what she knew about whirlwinds.

"You mean tornadoes?" said Zorrie.

"Whirlwinds," said Noah. "Like in the Bible and old stories. Like what Virgil says is starting to happen over there in Europe and the Pacific. Like what I get going in my head sometimes."

She thought carefully. "A whirlwind's a powerful force," she finally said.

Noah nodded. The sunlight coming over Zorrie's shoulder shone full on his face. His hair swept back in dark wet wings off his forehead, and his eyes were very blue.

"My wife's been writing me about them," he said. He reached into his hip pocket and pulled out a piece of paper that had clearly been folded and unfolded a considerable number of times.

"This is about one that hits the farm. The way she describes it, just about everything is whooshing around. Cats and pies and tomato plants. The place our house used to stand that now lies over yonder in that clover field. She writes me pretty frequent."

"Do you write her back?"

"I try to. Virgil helps. But they won't take the letters."

"Who won't? You mean the hospital?"

"Won't let me up to see her anymore either. Her family signed papers say I can't."

"I thought it was Virgil."

"That was to get her up there in the first place. That was his part. After she set the fire. That was bad enough."

"But Opal's your wife."

"I know it. It's others that don't."

Noah put the letter back in his pocket and left his hand in there with it. "I'm sorry about what you and Harold lost, Zorrie," he said after a moment.

Zorrie, surprised by this sudden shift in the conversation, opened her mouth to thank him, and then stopped. Looking at Noah, she felt something that had been held tight as wound baling twine inside her all summer loosen and her breaths started to come fast and shallow. She nodded, pressed her lips tight together, and wrapped her arms around herself. As she hurried away through the corn, the image of a bamboo fishing pole caught up in a whirlwind came along with her.

A YEAR PASSED. A second. A third. They tried but couldn't get another baby to take hold. Harold began to speak about the war differently. He went to basic training, then to Europe to serve as a navigator in the air force in the fall of 1942. Gus and Bessie moved back out to the farm with the idea that Gus would oversee the daily operations and Bessie would keep Zorrie company, but Gus was too worn out, as he put it, to do much in the way of overseeing, and Bessie spent the better part of the afternoons and evenings in bed. Zorrie, who for some time had been carrying about as much of the load on the farm as Harold, put Gus in charge of the stock, Bessie in charge of the kitchen, and hired on Lester Dunn to help in the fields because Noah had his hands full helping Virgil. Lester came early, worked hard, ate all the pie Bessie would feed him, and spoke rarely. He had a flair for finding mushrooms and sometimes, before he set out to join Zorrie, left a pail full by the door, which Bessie fried up with eggs, potatoes, and onions for dinner.

Harold sent letters to Gus and Bessie, which Gus read aloud at the kitchen table after supper, and to Zorrie, which she took up to bed with her and read over and over again by lamplight, trying and failing to picture Harold's distant hand and arm and eyes moving back and forth across the page. She kept them in the cigar box with the old clock face and Janie's letter and what was left of the powder. Two or three times a day she would open the box, pull out a letter, and read a few lines. At night she would let the box sit open and once even spilled out a little more of the remaining Luna powder so that she could see the pages glow. One, in which Harold attempted to describe the differences between Belgian and American ears of corn, was a particular favorite. More than any of the others, even the one where Harold described the sensation of riding in a "great machine that is going to take you speeding out over the dark Channel and the dark country beyond," it seemed to Zorrie to be imbued with some trace of its sender, some hint of the man she had lain and worked and fought against the snow beside, the man who had picked her up and swung her around. Still, it bothered her that the letters did so little to offset his absence. She had expected them to help more, to reduce the fear her mind had begun to fill up with. Thinking of Noah, she tried carrying them around with her, unfolding them on her tractor, in the barn, in the churchyard, under the south eaves on a rainy morning, beside the hickories in the small, sad autumn light. She tried keeping one crumpled up in her fist, another close to her heart. Frustrated, she spoke to Bessie about it, told her that no matter how brightly the letters glowed, they had all gone blurry, and she could barely see them or the man who had written them. Bessie sighed, asked Zorrie to fluff the pillow behind her, and said the only thing that would help was for Harold to drop out of the sky on a parachute and walk back in through the front door.

"I don't think he's ever going to," said Zorrie.

"Oh, hush now, he'll be back soon enough," Bessie said.

"No," said Zorrie, sitting down on the edge of the bed and letting her hands fall limp in her lap. "No, I don't think so."

Harold was killed in December 1943 off the coast of Holland when the final engine of the B-17 Flying Fortress he had served upon failed after sustaining heavy fire during a night raid on German artillery positions. The United States Air Force sent back his belongings, an honorary uniform, a medal and accompanying certificate, and the start of a letter written two days before his death.

> *My Darling Zorrie,*
> *It is ten days since I last wrote you, but that was only because they have been keeping us busy and not because I have not been thinking about you like I always do. Thank you for the*

*photograph of you standing by "the fields in November." You
and home is all I can think about. I wish you were here with
me and we could walk together through this countryside, where
even now, when it is so cold, the grass smells like flowers.*

Memorial services were held at both Hillisburg and Forest.
Bessie could not get out of bed to attend them and asked only
that they be sure to read the Twenty-Third Psalm. Gus tried
to make a speech at Hillisburg and read a poem at Forest, but
he didn't get far with either. Zorrie asked Virgil to say a few
words at Hillisburg. He wove John Adams, Thoreau, and
Emily Dickinson into remarks that many said afterward had
far outstripped Reverend Carter's. Ruby sang "Amazing
Grace," and Laetitia Bunch sang "The Old Wooden Cross."
Noah, dressed in a dark suit, sat very still throughout the
proceedings. When, at both churches, everyone else had sung
or spoken, Zorrie stood, thanked the congregation, then sat
back down and put a hand over her eyes.

The night after the second service, Zorrie dreamed that
she was back at her aunt's house, sitting in the darkened front
room sewing, and couldn't get the stitch right. She tried and
tried while her aunt stood over her, shaking her head. After
what seemed like hours of this, Zorrie woke, reached for
Harold, and gave a strangled cry.

Then the years sped past.

III

no shining roof or glittering window

B essie died in her sleep one spring morning in 1954. Gus did the same less than a year later. Zorrie was the only beneficiary named in his will. She took the proceeds from the sale of the house in Forest, made a donation to the church, then bought herself twenty acres of fallow land that Rupert Duff had put up for sale. She hired extra help and immediately put the field under cultivation. Two months after she had purchased it, bright green sprouts were pushing up through the black furrows.

As a general rule, Zorrie set to work before her help arrived and didn't stop until after they'd left. With Gus and Bessie no longer around to drop by and check up on her, she pushed even harder. More than once she fell asleep sitting on the tractor and woke later shivering and covered with mosquito bites. She grew so lean for a time that Ruby asked whenever she saw her if she was all right. Ruby had her own worries.

Virgil, always so eloquent, had fallen slowly into silence and was often found out wandering the woods and fields, unable to remember where he was. Ruby had tried putting reminder notes in his pockets, but it didn't help. She found them scattered throughout the house, across the yard, floating in the birdbath, under his pillow. If no one was watching him, he wandered off and didn't know the way home.

Zorrie saw him one day as she was plowing the back field. She had been daydreaming, not doing her best job, wondering what Lester would think of the mess she was making, when she spotted Virgil standing motionless by a maple stump near the ditch. She couldn't convince him to get on the tractor, so she climbed down, took him by the elbow, and led him home. Noah, who was trimming a hickory in his east woods, walked out across the field to meet them. He thanked Zorrie and then put his hand on Virgil's shoulder. Watching them walk away together, it struck Zorrie that the silence that rode the air between them was a comfortable one. For just a moment, she thought how nice it would be to walk in their company, or, better, to just float quietly between them, caught on a forward-tending gust of air. Then she turned around, went back to her tractor, and climbed on.

In the months after Harold's death, after Gus and Bessie had at her insistence moved back to Forest, when Harold seemed to be standing just around every corner she turned, and the repeated realization that he wasn't standing anywhere, not even on French, Dutch, or English soil, let alone somewhere on the farm, set her to pacing the hallways of the house for nights entire, she had thrown herself at the ever-present acreage around her with all the strength she could muster. She took to countering every thought of Harold's physical erasure with an image, as quickly made actual, of her arms hefting a hoe, a bag of seed, a bale, a well-sharpened scythe. How the horse-weed fell that first summer! She would speak about Harold if the subject was raised but would suffer for it afterward, and did her best never to bring the ongoing fact of his absence up to herself outside the formulas of nightly prayer. The crisply chiseled tale of time told by the clocks and watches she had once helped paint faces for came to seem complicit in the agonized unfolding of her grief, so that soon the farm and the surrounding fields and the endless ark of change that enclosed them were the only timepiece whose hour strokes she could abide. Small but sure of purpose within the great mechanism of the seasons, she became a pin on a barrel of wind, a screw in a dial of sunlight, a tooth on an escape wheel of rain. The crops went in, the crops were cared for, the crops came out. The earth rested in its right season, and she with it. If the ache of Harold's absence descended on her during the quiet months, she would take a rag to it with her mind and rub.

Over the years, this approach so drastically diminished the frequency with which Zorrie thought of Harold that she eventually worried there might be some fault in it, especially because now when he was mentioned by one of her neighbors or she chanced upon an undiscovered fishing lure or belt buckle she hadn't yet learned how not to notice, the burn that had always hit her at the back of the chest was gone. This lack of any painful reaction—a lack she had so longed for—struck her, now that it had arrived, as too complete. It made her feel she had taken it all too far. You came to terms with things, but not by carrying them out to the field and burying them under the beans. Mr. Thomas had long ago told her class that "the encumbering elements of our histories must be spoken aloud, at least in the caverns of our brains, if we wish for them to take up wings." Remembering this as she thumbed through a volume of Longfellow at Mary Thompson's estate sale, it occurred to Zorrie that there might be some compromise available in thinking not of Harold's death and absence, but of him.

She dug one of his watches out of a drawer, wound and set it, wore it loose and lightly ticking as she went about her chores. She turned her mind actively to remembering in the evenings. Occasionally she would hold his picture in front of her, or let her eyes glide over one of his letters, or pick up his fishing hat or coffee mug, but usually she just sat there and eventually saw him, with a clarity that relieved her, walking across the barn lot, or standing, shoulders slumped, hands plunged deep in his pockets, head thrown back, or striding through the clover with a tire iron in his hand, or running the tractor across the open field, or slinging the rifle over his shoulder and heading for the woods. It was not uncommon in these moments that other images—some directly related, others related only in that they belonged to Zorrie's past— interposed themselves: the towheaded Kelly twins working a cat's cradle in the school yard, Zorrie's aunt frowning as she canned peaches, Gus getting angry over cards, a young couple at a long-ago Fourth of July picnic looking hungrily into each other's eyes, Mr. Thomas walking through the woods, pointing at leaves with the same ruler he used in the class-room, Janie's hand reaching for the powder-filmed bowl of red hots next to her basket of dials, Noah biting into an apple or reading aloud from one of Opal's letters or staring out across the fields. Sounds, smells, and tastes came and attached themselves to the pictures she saw: old leaves rustling as she and Harold moved through the underbrush in search of a picnic spot, the big smell of Mrs. Thomas and her cohort on a blazing August afternoon, the mineral-sweet taste of warm blackberries picked off the vines along the back fence. During daylight hours, when she was bent over the spinach or feeding the chickens or going over some point of business with Lester, she called herself foolish or self-indulgent for dwelling on the past. But more and more, as the air grew cooler, evening came on, and the night, with Harold's watch wound to neatly mark it, stretched ahead, she became aware that the past, what her aunt had called "nothing but a tinker's circus of two-bit shadows," and what she had worked so long to forget, was where she felt most at ease.

One night, though, after she had spent hours revisiting the first days of her courtship with Harold, when she had been meant to look over equipment prospectuses, she woke with a start from a half sleep and saw Harold leaning in the doorway, looking at her. She shut her eyes, and when she opened them he was gone, but then the air beside her ear grew cold and she shivered and she heard Harold say, "I'm hungry, Zorrie. It's been years since I ate anything. You've got to give me some food."

That was a dream, Zorrie thought. I wasn't awake yet. But her ear still felt like it had spent time in the icebox, and there was a damp smell to the air. Harold's watch had stopped, but instead of rewinding it, she yanked it off her wrist and, all but gasping, tossed it back in the drawer. Later, after she had gotten her breathing back to normal, and her mind had set the door of her world more or less back on its hinges, it struck her that, worse than getting carried away, she was losing control. Complicating matters was the fact that she couldn't decide if the prospect felt agreeable or unpleasant or both.

She thought about it for days. She was short with Lester and sent Earl off in search of a set of scales she told him was in the barn but that, in fact, she had taken to the dump years before. She saw Lloyd Duff at the bank and didn't recognize him at first because the wrinkled and crook-shouldered figure who stood endorsing a check on the other side of the lobby looked almost nothing like the image of the younger man she had seen chuckling in a group with Harold during one of her recent reveries. When he looked up and said, "Well, there's our farming gal, Zorrie," it was a long moment before she was able to answer, and on her way out she stumbled on the lintel, flailed her arms for balance, and almost fell into a hedge. "You're not decrepit yet, so quit acting like it," she said aloud to herself.

But the next day she forgot to feed the chickens, burned her breakfast, made another mess of plowing, and dreamed that night about flightless jays and silences and floating through the air. She woke disoriented and sweating in an early light laced by dream residue and thought of Virgil and Noah. The next morning, shivering as she walked along the fencerows and negotiated jagged bean stubble, she went to look for them. She found Noah, saw in hand, in the branches of the same hickory he had been trimming the day before. Virgil, wrapped in a bright blue scarf and a winter coat, sat on a low stool under an enormous black oak.

"You're getting this tree into shape," she said.

"It's either that or lose it," said Noah.

"You need any help hauling branches?"

"Just going to pile them up and light a match."

"I could help pile."

"I bet you got your own work."

"I do."

Noah leaned into the tree, his wrinkled brown coveralls blending in with the trunk's dark crenellations. He looked down at her, then closed his eyes, lifted a gloved hand to his mouth, caught his breath, pulled a gulp of air into his lungs, and sneezed.

"Bless you," said Zorrie.

"Virgil never liked that," said Noah. "He says that blessing a sneeze is like taking up a shotgun to attend to a fly. He's got a German word he likes to say when there's a sneeze. Well, when he was saying things."

Zorrie looked at Virgil, who appeared to be dozing.

"He's not asleep," Noah said.

Zorrie nodded.

"He hears us. He's hearing me right now. I just don't know where my voice goes when it gets in past his ear. Maybe all the words fall and just keep falling."

Zorrie said maybe that was so.

"I wonder what it's like to have words falling through your head."

"Nice, I hope."

Noah looked over at Virgil, shook his head, said he wasn't sure. He said he thought maybe it was words that tripped a person up in the first place. Words in free fall couldn't be a good thing, especially if, as in Virgil's case, they were falling through so much quiet, when before there'd been so much talk.

Zorrie didn't say anything. A heavy truck went by on the road. Small mechanical sounds drifted across the fields. Noah coughed and asked Zorrie if she would like him to climb down from the tree.

Yes, I would, Zorrie thought. That is exactly what I would like. She thought of everything she'd planned to say as she walked around the house, waiting for the birds to start up: that the past seemed to have sprung itself on her just when she thought she was clear of it; that all she'd wanted was to think about Harold a little, bring him back to her, and then the whole old ugly clockworks had come crashing down on her in a jumble of gears and springs; that she wanted to plop herself onto the cold, crumpled grass near the two of them and just sit there and not move; that there were dark roses and pigs and dead husbands and throat-torn fish in her whirlwind of a head.

She sighed. "No," she said. "I should get back. Thank you. I was just out taking a turn."

As she walked away, she stepped on a wet branch hidden under a gathering of oak leaves. The surprisingly loud snap made her start and sent a pair of nuthatches flicking off through the gray air around the black oak. Virgil didn't seem to notice.

"Next I'll step in a well," she said, waving over her shoulder and hurrying off.

"Don't do that, Zorrie Underwood," Noah said.

Her aunt had disparaged the concept of hope with such caustic efficiency that Zorrie had naturally learned to discount what had ever been an important part of her nature. If she had done her best to seal up the spring during those early years and then again after Harold's death, hope had nonetheless often found a way to seep out and surprise her, bow graciously, extend its hand, and ask her to dance. It had done so when she had knocked on the door in Jefferson and found Mr. Thomas with his plums and iced tea and albums standing before her, and it had done so when Gus had decided he liked the way she whistled, and spoke to Bessie about their spare room. Hope had also, certainly, flapped its fair wings for her when a man with a sandwich to share had told her about jobs to be had in Ottawa. She had occasion to think of this later that day when she opened her mailbox and saw that a postcard had been set to lean in the shadows against its rusty wall. It took her a moment to recognize the picture, which showed a train car on what looked like an iron bridge. On the back was printed "Chicago's Famous 'L.'" There was a hole at the top where the tack had held it to the wall. The tack had been brass-colored. Zorrie could remember touching at its smooth head with her finger more than a few times. As she read and reread the note scrawled in Janie's riotously looping hand, she understood that she was holding one of those rare objects brought into being by a hope you didn't know you still had.

> *Took me a while but I finally got up there. How about you, Ghost Girl? You take a ride on your own L yet?*

Zorrie planned it out early the next morning—she would drive herself north to the great city, where she could walk along Michigan Avenue and gaze upon the giant buildings and look in the shop windows and step into Marshall Field's and ride a screaming train through the sky. Then she would head down to Ottawa and see Janie and Marie and tell them about it and learn what they had done with themselves over the years and visit with some of the other girls. Maybe even some of the boys. Show them the sprinklings of gray she was getting. See if they'd had any early winter sky settling down on them too. Laugh with them about too little sleep and too much thinking that made you forget things. They were all older, but they could still paint themselves in Luna powder if they wanted, could still walk out through the quiet streets and stand luminous under the stars. She told Lester to look after things, that she would be gone for a few days, maybe even a week. The distant months she had spent in Ottawa danced before her eyes as she drove first east then north up past Lafayette, Monticello, and Rensselaer. She'd recently had new tires put on her truck, and if the old engine complained about the unaccustomed speed Zorrie was encouraging it to achieve, the tires hummed and sang as the towns and fields blurred by.

It began raining near Demotte, and she discovered she needed new wipers. When she found herself in Valparaiso instead of Merrillville, she knew she had gotten turned around. She got gas, fresh wipers, and directions at a filling station, but either the directions were bad or she hadn't listened closely enough because pretty soon she was at Woodville, then Porter, and instead of passing signs for Chicago, she was seeing signs for Lake Michigan and the Indiana Dunes. She went as far as the road would take her and ended up in a parking lot nestled against high hills of sand. She got out and walked up a trail. The sand made it feel like she was walking through molasses. It even stuck to her shoes as if it were as syrupy as it felt. The rain had stopped and left a thick mist behind. She thought she might as well go as far as Lake Michigan before she got herself steered back in the right direction.

The dunes stretched all around, as far as the mist would let her see. Little wind-harassed trees grew here and there, and the dunes were covered with long grass and did not look like the pictures she had seen in *Life* magazine of their great cousins in the Sahara Desert. Gulls called overhead. There was no one else around. The sand never stopped moving. She bent over and dragged a finger through it. In places it was damp and in others dry. She took up a pinch between her fingers and saw that not only were the grains different colors, they were also different sizes. Some of the bigger grains were rose-colored, a few appeared almost violet, and she wished she had better light and a magnifying glass. She tossed what she was holding into the air. The sand rode out and then down in a wind-feathered arc that pleased her so much she did it again. Standing there, she realized she could smell the lake, had been smelling it for some time. The smell seemed strange and bottomless and gave her a pang in her stomach she couldn't put a name to. She had heard Lake Michigan was very beautiful. Bessie and Gus had taken Harold camping on its shores once. She started to move again, hoping soon to hit water, sand crunching and pillowing underfoot. She felt sure she was getting close when it started to hail. All she could think to do, besides bury herself in the dunes, was head back to the truck. The sound of the small white pellets striking the sand was wonderfully muted, and if they hadn't started to hurt as they hit against her, she might have stopped to more carefully listen.

Once safe inside the cab of her truck, she thought that since it wasn't even midday yet, she would wait it out and take another try at reaching the lake, but when the hail turned into more rain she put the key in the ignition. The engine started slowly, sounded tired when it did catch, and it coughed twice as she was pulling out of the lot. One of her sweet new tires took a nail before she had a chance to turn west out of Porter. Though she got the tire changed without trouble, she ended up soaked and chilled and wondering what to do next. The simple yellow town dress with a worn lace collar she had tossed in her bag to put on in Ottawa when she was with her old friends wasn't the kind of thing you could wear out on Michigan Avenue, she thought, much less into Marshall Field's. The pang made itself felt again in her stomach. It was for the deep water she had smelled but hadn't glimpsed, she now understood. She didn't get anything like the same feeling when she thought of Janie's L, though she believed she might if she actually took a ride on it. I'll give it a try another day, she thought, though she wasn't sure whether she meant Chicago or the lake. An image of her aunt, making her hold out her hand so it could be struck with a spatula because she'd said she hoped it would be sunny the next day, floated up before her. It had not been sunny the next day. "Hope'll lead you straight into the bushes. Look where hope led me," her aunt had said. The hills of sand had been beautiful, so that was something. There was always something. Even when there wasn't. In her mind's eye she saw again the shape the grains had made as they flew from her fingers, then tried to imagine the shape Harold's smoking plane might have made as it fell through the distant Dutch skies. Condensation had formed on the inside of the truck's windshield, and she traced an arc that was either the sand or Harold or both. The L would roar without wavering over and over again through the air, she thought, and traced a great loop. But what shape would she make? She traced small ripples, then larger waves, then a spiral, then a well that was all sides and no bottom—like the one where Virgil's words had gone or the place where Noah's Opal now lived—but this made her shiver, so she rubbed it out. Suddenly she felt very tired. She ran a hand through all she had drawn, and then put the truck into drive again.

THE FOLLOWING EVENING Ruby called Zorrie up and asked if she was done traipsing around the countryside. A few minutes later she knocked on the door and handed Zorrie a box containing a purple blanket and a jet-black puppy curled up and snoring so lightly that Zorrie thought maybe she was imagining it.

"Johnsons had a litter they were getting rid of, so I had Noah run over there and get you one," Ruby said.

Zorrie looked at the box, then at Ruby.

"You need company," Ruby said.

"I never had a dog."

"Now you do."

"We always had cats around."

"Cats are different."

"How?"

"Just different. There's nothing spooky about a dog."

"Well," said Zorrie.

"It needs a name," Ruby said.

Zorrie put a hand into the box and brushed her finger against a stomach the size of a large russet potato and tight as a balloon. The puppy blinked open an eye, shut it again as fast, curled up its spine, stretched out its paws, and recommenced snoring. Zorrie had just been reading an article about the benefits of switching over to a strict corn-beans-clover rotation and had been wondering if she should give up the ten acres she still put out in oats, which hadn't done her much good for some years. She touched the puppy's stomach again and then asked Ruby what it ate.

"Scraps and bread mush. More or less whatever you got."

"How often?"

"Mornings and evenings, to get started. You got any other questions, you can ask Noah—he had a dog."

"I didn't know that."

"What are you going to call it?"

"Oats," said Zorrie.

Zorrie invited Ruby in for a cup of hot cocoa, but Ruby said she had to get home and see what her men were getting themselves up to. She had just wanted to deliver the pup and give Zorrie something to think about that wasn't more than a few weeks old. She said she understood Zorrie had been having trouble nights.

"Yes," said Zorrie.

"I expect nights are the hardest when you're living alone."

"You talked to Noah."

"He talked to me. Said you'd been having dreams, seeing things."

"I never told him that. In fact I never got around to telling him anything at all."

"Well, are you?

"Yes."

"You ought to come over more. Come up to the house and visit. It's not Chicago, but it's not the inside of your four walls either. Neither one of us is any great shakes at reading, and that's about the only thing that'll keep Virgil in his chair of an evening. You get this Oats figured out, then come over and have supper with us and read. We'd all enjoy it."

OATS SLEPT A good deal, soiled the towels Zorrie spread out in a corner of the back porch, frequently tripped over her feet, ate with appetite, barked at everything, especially birds, displayed a predilection for fussing in Zorrie's lap and chewing on her buttons, and just generally insinuated herself into a great amount of Zorrie's time. Noah stopped by every few days to pick Oats up, cradle her against his chest, and let her lick his face. Zorrie said she didn't necessarily like a dog that licked. Noah said, "Well, this here Oats is one that does."

Zorrie started taking her supper with the Summerses on Thursdays. Ruby would serve entirely too much good food, and then they would go into the living room and Zorrie would read. It was true that Virgil, who throughout the meal would have stood up and started to wander off any number of times, never budged from his seat whenever she opened a book. He seemed, in fact, almost attentive when she read from one of his old stacks: the letters of John Adams or Montaigne's essays or Herodotus or Cicero or Aeschylus. While Ruby perked up considerably when Zorrie took up the Bible and read passages from the Gospels or the Psalms, Virgil's attention, such as it was, seemed at those moments to drop off, and more than once Zorrie was convinced that he had fallen asleep, that the words had returned to plummeting down their bottomless hole. For his part, Noah sat perched on a handmade wooden chair behind his parents and always listened with great focus to whatever Zorrie read.

It was certainly the case that between these evenings and the antics of her new charge, Zorrie found herself dwelling less, and soon there were no more nightmares and apparitions. If she sometimes turned to sad memories of the winter evenings she and Harold had read to each other, or thought of her failure even at the simple task of driving north, she found the feelings tempered by thoughts of the Summerses' living room—with its neat furniture, the painting of deep-blue cornflowers above the fireplace, and the long-since-broken barometer next to the pie safe—by Ruby and Virgil and Noah, by the blanket of good silence that surrounded her as she read. Handwritten into the margin of Virgil's copy of Montaigne, next to the dog-eared opening of the essay on sadness, were the words "The fragile film of the present must be buttressed against the past," and Zorrie found herself turning to this page, just to let her eyes run over it, every time she picked up the book. When Noah asked Zorrie why she did this, Zorrie said it reminded her of something her old teacher had liked to cite, only she liked Virgil's—if it was Virgil's—twist to it better. Ruby said the note had indeed been written by Virgil and that it certainly sounded like something he would come up with. Noah agreed. He said Virgil had read the essay to him again and again during his bad spells after Opal had been taken, not least, Noah supposed, because it contained a line by Virgil's namesake: "And grief at long hard last breaks a way for the voice." Noah said that in truth he had always been partial to the next citation, by Petrarch: "He who can say how he burns, burns little."

"I like that very much," said Zorrie. "Do you suppose it's true?"

"Maybe it depends on how you're burning," Noah said.

"Let's not talk too much about burning," Ruby said with a shiver.

Zorrie wondered aloud if Montaigne really had been as free from sadness as he claimed, and Noah said he highly doubted it, but wished he could ask Virgil, who seemed, at that moment, to be listening to something off in the distance while staring straight through the south wall.

"That there man is my sadness," said Ruby, who then shifted in her seat and remarked that it was all handsome notions, but if they didn't mind she'd just as soon converse about something else.

Warmer weather came, and Oats spent her days defending the territory. She'd bark at anything that moved and worked at developing her growl. After a time she seemed to have made her peace with the birds, but squirrels were another matter entirely. If a squirrel set foot on any part of the yard, Oats was after it like one of the furies of old. It seemed to Zorrie that she spent a good deal longer than was necessary standing at the base of trees, her feet set wide, ears pulled back, barking. Whenever the coast was clear, which it was more and more as the squirrels took their business out to the woods, Oats would snuffle around in the bushes, chase butterflies, or nap with a fair amount of rolling and whining on the piece of red carpet Zorrie had set out by the back door. Generally, when Zorrie came back from the fields at noon or in the evening,

Oats would run out to the end of the lane to greet her, and when Zorrie got out of the truck, she'd jump up and leave paw prints on her overalls and see how many times her tongue could make significant contact with Zorrie's face.

With summer, though, Oats took to wandering. Zorrie saw and heard her barking all over the farm and surrounding fields. Sometimes she wouldn't turn up for her supper, and more often than not when she did, she'd be filthy and covered in burs. One evening Ethel Duff, who lived near Pickard, drove over with Oats in the back seat of her Ford. At church, Candy Wilson announced that she'd spotted Zorrie's "young criminal" eyeballing her chickens.

"There's people who'll shoot a roaming dog, even if they know who it belongs to," Reverend Carter said, with just a touch too much endorsement of the idea in his tone.

Zorrie consulted Lester, who counseled a firm hand in all matters related to domestic animals, and took a book on raising dogs out of the library. This book stressed the importance, for character, of pedigree. Fred Johnson told Zorrie that Oats's father was a pointer-mix hellion who'd drifted through more than once. The mother, she could inspect for herself. This mother had some beagle to her and, apart from an undeniable malodorous quality that fortunately hadn't manifested in the daughter, was personable enough to wag her tail and nuzzle Zorrie's hand, though she didn't display a tremendous amount of alacrity when Fred called on her to perform a trick about "shaking paws."

"She bark at squirrels?" Zorrie asked.

"I've seen the father at that. But this one does like to wander. That's the beagle facet. She made it over to Tipton once. Fortunately, I'd put the tags on her. She's cooled off somewhat now that she's older."

"I have to wait until Oats is older for her to stop running around the countryside?"

"Well, every dog's a different customer, but if she keeps it up, I understand they have a college or some such over at Frankfort that's supposed to help their comportment."

"College?" said Zorrie.

But when the mailman said he'd seen Oats halfway to Scircleville carrying what looked like the leftovers of a rabbit in her mouth, she stopped by Barb's Dog College and took a brochure.

"Escort her in here," said Barb. "We'll get her trained up."

Barb gave a whistle, and a Great Dane the size of a donkey came in and sat politely.

"This individual was formerly a cushion chewer," she said. "Now this individual is not. We got guaranteed results."

Zorrie likely would have enrolled Oats (or at the least taken Candy Wilson's suggestion that she get some more fencing, or a good long piece of rope), if, apparently as she was wandering back by the ditch, Oats hadn't made the acquaintance of Virgil.

Ruby told Zorrie about it as they ate wilted lettuce together one Thursday evening. She'd gone out looking for Virgil on Monday and found the pair of them sitting in some tall grass under a maple near the ditch. When she got Virgil up and started walking him back, Oats had come along and hadn't left when Ruby sat Virgil down in his chair by the side door. She had just sat there quietly until her suppertime, then got up, licked Virgil's hand, and headed home.

"The next morning," Ruby said, "she was waiting by his chair. And she's spent the day with him ever since."

"I hope she's not causing any trouble," said Zorrie.

"No, and I'll tell you something else, he doesn't get up to his own tricks when she's around. Or anyway, fewer tricks let's say."

Ruby crossed her arms, and Noah leaned forward. "I found them this afternoon out by that hickory tree where we talked that time," he said.

"What were they doing?"

"Just sitting."

All three of them looked over at Virgil, who was spooning wilted lettuce with at best moderate success toward his mouth. Noah got up, went over to the window, and then came back and nodded.

"She's out there right now, lying by the chair."

Once or twice the next week, Zorrie drove by the Summerses' during the day and saw Oats curled up in the shade next to Virgil. When the following Thursday Ruby confirmed that she hadn't missed a day, Zorrie stopped worrying. As they walked home together after Zorrie had put Ruby, Virgil, and, she suspected, even Noah to sleep reading from a book on the life of James Whitcomb Riley, which had included long selections of his verse, Zorrie pulled a piece of ham loaf she'd saved in a napkin from her pocket, gave it to Oats with a pat, and said there'd be more if she kept behaving herself.

Oats became such a fixture at the Summerses' side door during the daytime that when she didn't appear one morning in late September, Ruby went as far as the lane calling for her, and so did not see Virgil, who had gotten out of his chair and gone back into the house, take his last breath and fall over in the kitchen. It was Noah, she told Zorrie the next evening as they sat together in the Summerses' kitchen, who had found him. After Ruby had given up calling Oats (who as far as Zorrie could tell had spent the day sitting quietly on her red mat at home), she had gotten distracted by some weeds fringing her squash and had come back to find Noah cradling his dead father's head in his arms.

"It was hard to tell which one of them was quieter," Ruby said. Noah hadn't left his room since the ambulance had come the day before and taken Virgil away. He needed to eat or at least drink something. She knew he didn't have any water up there. Zorrie said she expected Noah was deeply upset, and that this was his way of tending to it. Ruby said that he hadn't been too upset to get up to some of his foolishness before the ambulance had arrived. Zorrie raised an eyebrow and looked at her. Ruby pointed at the carpet by the door to the washroom where Virgil had fallen, and said she still had more scrubbing to do. Zorrie tilted her head and could see the borders of a faint white oval on the green carpet. The space inside the oval looked so small she couldn't quite believe it had gone all the way around Virgil.

"I'd of put a stop to it if I wasn't sure it was something the two of them cooked up at some point. You know the kind of things Virgil liked to read, and a lot of those things got communicated into Noah's head. A ring of lime powder around his father. My glory. It was probably something to do with some old battle procedure or similar monkey business. I don't know what all he'll get up to when I'm gone."

Zorrie took Ruby's hand, put her arm around her shoulder, and held her until she had quieted. Then she went upstairs and knocked on Noah's door. There was a silence, and Zorrie knocked again.

"You in there?" she asked.

"I am, Zorrie Underwood," said Noah, his voice slightly muffled by the door.

"Your mother's upset and could use some company. I've been down there with her."

"Thank you."

"And I expect you could use something to eat. She said you haven't been out of this room since yesterday. Can I bring you up a plate and a glass of water?"

Noah didn't answer. Zorrie leaned closer to the door. She had never been in his room, had never given much thought to his having one. Her mind offered up a strangely vivid series of images—a simple chair by a small window, a poster bed under the eaves, a closet hung with clean shirts, a large, scarred hand aswim in yellow lamplight—as she leaned her cheek against the cool wood. When Noah spoke again, Zorrie realized that either the room was very small or he was standing very close to her.

"She knew," Noah said. "That dog of yours. She had it figured."

"Well," said Zorrie. "I expect she did."

"I didn't. Didn't have any idea about it. I didn't know until he had hit the floor. I heard it from the barn."

"Well," said Zorrie.

"There was a dead moth on the eave, and it shook and thumped while I was looking at it, and I knew he was dead."

Zorrie couldn't quite tell from Noah's voice, which seemed both deeper and tighter to her than usual, if he was crying or not. She decided he was.

"The green mark," Noah said.

"What?" Zorrie said.

"He told me a long time ago he'd show me the green mark before it was over, and he did."

"What does the green mark mean?"

"I don't know. Death, I suppose. Life, mystery. Mostly mystery."

Zorrie saw again the faint oval on the green carpet and shivered. Small as it had been, it seemed linked in her mind to the gigantic lake, lost in mist, that she hadn't been able to get her eyes on. She thought of Noah standing at the edge of the field years before, holding a letter in his hand and talking about whirlwinds in his head. She thought of him standing with a saw in his hand, talking about falling and falling, and she thought about Virgil lying somewhere in Frankfort, waiting to be lowered into the ground. She thought about Harold falling through the sky and Opal sitting in an ice bath and Mrs. Thomas eating carrot stubs out of her hand. She thought of Noah standing over the fire at the Fourth of July picnic, thought of his long arms in the red light, thought of Oats and her red carpet, thought of Noah, crying no more than two feet away from her, thought of her arms going out like they had for Ruby, thought, I am thinking more than I need to, and I ought to get home.

"Anyway, I wanted to let you know your mother could use your company," she said, pulling her ear away from the door.

"Thank you, Zorrie. It was a service. I'll get down there before long."

"Are you going to be all right?"

Noah didn't answer. Zorrie turned, took a step, heard the door opening behind her, stopped.

"You ought to have this," Noah said, his voice even deeper and tighter than it had seemed hidden behind the inch or so of door. He was standing barely lit by the hall light, holding out the tattered copy of Montaigne with both hands. Zorrie didn't move. The room behind him was dark, cavelike. The air that had come out with him smelled of lemons and shoe polish. Zorrie could see traces of wet in the pale creases on Noah's cheeks.

"You know I can't take that. That's yours and Ruby's."

"What was ours fell over into his green mark. Just like your Harold fell into his. Ruby's been saying she wanted you to have it. And I've figured for a while Virgil would have wanted it to be yours."

Zorrie pictured Harold hitting green water, his burned and broken plane sinking down through the green dark. To drift or settle? To rise? To have his bones gnawed by small, sharp mouths? By the fragile film of the present? Of the past? Which was it? Weren't you supposed to be able to read a message once it had been sent? She shivered and shook her head, but reached forward, took the book the way it was offered, with both her hands. Their fingers didn't touch but came very close. She asked again if Noah was going to be all right, and again Noah didn't answer, just thanked her, wiped his forearm across his cheek, and wished her good night. A few minutes later, hurrying away from the house with the green roof down the green lane toward the green woods and home, with nothing but unanswerable mysteries alongside her, Zorrie decided it would have been strange if he had.

Oats was waiting for her under the forsythia bush. Zorrie brought her into the kitchen and gave her half a burned pork chop left over from lunch and poured herself a glass of milk. Some of the milk slopped over the edge of the glass when she set it down on the counter. She started to get a cloth, but stopped, lifted the glass, and took a drink. Oats licked her lips, lifted her ears, and whined. Zorrie gave her the rest of the pork chop, took another drink, said, "Hush now," wondered who, exactly, she was saying it to, opened the copy of Virgil's Montaigne, read a moment, closed it, and then stood there a long time, staring down at her hands.

IV

this Palace seems light as a cloud set for a moment in the sky

S easons of flood, of fine weather, of fair harvest, of drought. September storms in the late 1950s took down two of Zorrie's elephant oaks so she put in pawpaws, and when those didn't make it she settled on maple and hickory and watched with pleasure as they began to grow sturdy and make their shapes in the air. She had the flu one year, three colds the next, and then wasn't sick the following two. On balance, the farm did well enough to make it worth investing in a second grain bin. Her old truck gave up the ghost, so she got herself a new one. After the county forced her to slaughter her few remaining hogs because of a swine virus that was making the rounds, she stopped raising stock. It had been one thing to kill those brave, smart creatures for their meat, but quite another to tractor-shove their shot carcasses into the earth. There were other compensations, though. She had put out butterfly bushes, and the air filled up. Wrens and robins and downy woodpeckers fell in love with her woods. She found so many four-leaf clovers, she wore herself out cutting slips of waxed paper to press them in. Nobody at church or in town ever said no to slipping one into their purse or wallet, and Lester made a show of wearing the two she had given him in his hatband. Meanwhile, her ever-expanding garden flourished. She harvested far more than she could consume and, when she wasn't "handing out the luck," as Candy Wilson put it, got into the habit of sharing most of what she had canned and frozen with her neighbors, especially the less fortunate ones. Her big jars of ham and green beans were particularly welcome, as were her dill pickles. Everyone thought she had the recipe down just right.

One spring Sheriff Hank Dunn, who had been a few years ahead of Harold at school and had attended his memorial service at Hillisburg, took to paying Zorrie visits in the evening. The first time he came, it was to ask her to sign a petition on safety procedures being circulated by the volunteer fire department. The second time, three days later, it was to provide her with an update as well as supplementary information because he was just driving by. After he had left, Zorrie wasn't quite sure what she thought about his visit, much less his suggestion that he come by again the following week, but she did note that she had been bothered the whole time they stood out by his cruiser that she had been wearing a pair of filthy overalls and rubber field boots. The next time he came, she had on a pair of jeans and a clean yellow windbreaker, and the week after that, she paused a moment in front of the mirror before she walked out across the yard to greet him.

The first time he took her into town, they ate steaks, peas, and mashed potatoes with passable gravy and continued their driveway conversations about the vicissitudes of weather and high school basketball and crop yields and rural police work. Zorrie brought up some of her neighbors, including the Summerses, and Hank smiled. Hank had known Virgil well and spoke of him with great respect. His decline and death had robbed the community of one of its most consistently refreshing constituents. "I used to just stand there and listen to him, there wasn't anything like it. One time he got going about the achievements of Julius Caesar, or I don't know which one it was, and he went on, with about as much detail as if he'd been there gobbling the grapes down himself, for at least an hour. He knew everyone's names like he was talking about what was going on over at the Elks lodge. He got all worked up. I'm pretty sure he told me what they ate for breakfast. You couldn't beat it with a stick. Funny thing was, it never had a nickel to do with showing off." Hank leaned back in his chair and shook his head as if he was picturing it. Zorrie said that was the way she had always seen it too, then added that she wasn't sure Noah had felt the same.

"Hard to say," Hank said. "I've never known a son who admired his father more, that's the truth. But the truth there gets shipwrecked on the shores of their old family complaints. I know that remains the case. That Opal he lost is still more or less the blood beating through his veins."

Hank seemed to know three-quarters of the restaurant, so their conversation was interspersed with a fair number of greetings and light remarks and frequent interpellations from the elderly waitresses, who seemed always to be moving forward with pots of coffee or heavily laden plates in their hands. Zorrie enjoyed these interruptions, enjoyed how easily Hank moved his focus from one person to the next, how in consequence she could get in steady doses, which seemed more and more necessary the longer they sat there, of telling herself that there was nothing wrong with what she was doing, that in fact she wasn't doing anything at all, and that even if it *was* something, which it was not, it would be all right. Everything would be all right. It was just dinner. She was over fifty years old now. She was a big girl. Two of these dinners later, however, during a lull in a conversation about Pioneer versus Champion yields, Hank reached across the table, put his hand over hers, and squeezed gently. She did not react immediately, even smiled at him, rotated her hand, and squeezed back. But when a moment later she pulled her hand away, picked her napkin up off her lap, and said they had better go, she felt it with a finality that seemed in retrospect, as she sat on the porch that night with Oats breathing noisily beside her, to have been built into the proceedings from the moment Hank had pulled up in her driveway with his pretext and big laugh and pleasantness and easy words about the weather.

Hank himself helped Zorrie to confirm this hypothesis when he drove over the next evening, knocked on her door, accepted the glass of iced tea she handed him, and said, "I knew I didn't have a chance from day one."

"But you kept on."

Hank winked. "I thought it was worth it."

"Why? Why was it worth it?"

"I guess that'll be for someone else to explain to you, Zorrie. I've been dealt out."

Zorrie had thought of several things to say to Hank the next time she saw him, several approaches to elaborating on her request to be taken home, her suggestion as they pulled up in her driveway that it would be best and easiest if he didn't call on her again, at least not in the way he'd been doing. She had gone so far as to imagine herself taking his arm or touching his hand as she spoke to him, as she tried to explain things, standing out by his car or walking with him along the lane in the orange evening with the sun sliding down the sky. That there was very little substance to these imagined explanations, these glosses on feelings she didn't have more than the odd word or two for, seemed painfully obvious to her now under the bright kitchen lights, so she simply said what the better part of it boiled down to anyway: "I'm sorry, Hank."

"No sorry to it. Like I said, anyone could have seen you were thinking elsewhere. I just tend close enough toward stubborn to keep on even when I'm close to certain it won't do me any good. Which is fortunately not necessarily the worst trait to have when it comes to sheriffing."

Hank laughed, but not loudly and not for very long. Zorrie picked up her glass, looked at the sugary slush at its bottom, set it back down again, and said, "Elsewhere?"

They both looked out the window. There was a breeze running through the young leaves, making them shiver, and long shadows careened across the yard. Oats was off at the fencerow, barking and digging after something. In the summer the leaves and foliage would completely obscure the view, but now it was still possible to see a corner of the Summerses' green roof through the trees.

"Harold, Hank. My husband. If it's anywhere I'm looking, it's at his memory, at him."

"Of course. That's some of it, always will and should be. That part I had thought through. You said yourself you'd found some peace to that. A bushel full of years can do that for you."

Zorrie nodded. She had said something to that effect at one of their meals. And now she realized that she had meant it. Had felt it for some time now. When she called Harold to mind these days, what answered was mostly soft, like the few flecks of powder left to glow in the cigar box, and bore only the faintest resemblance to even the tatters of anything as big as longing.

"I suppose you know that's not what I meant," said Hank.

Zorrie started to protest, then stopped.

Hank smiled. "There's things that get half said plenty loud enough when we don't think about it. Things that slip through the cracks. Line items we got on our minds have a tendency to come out whether we know or like it."

"Well," said Zorrie.

"Yes, well, Zorrie, and I thank you sincerely for the tea and for all our nice talks and evenings," said Hank, nodding, standing, stepping towards the door.

All right, Zorrie thought, shrugging at the fact that her cheeks were burning, that they'd likely been bright apple red when she'd said her goodbye to Hank, then shrugging again when she said aloud to her empty kitchen, "So there it is, and even Hank Dunn knows it, and what good exactly will it do you?"

Precious little, it seemed to her over the coming weeks. In fact, the most significant outcome of this admission of what she understood was woven closely together with the slow shifting of her feelings about Harold was that, despite her concern about Ruby, who was swimming into the final stretch of her own silver stream, she found herself going down to the Summerses' less frequently than she had before, and that when she did, she wasn't always up to being what she felt was acceptable company. One evening as she was walking toward the house to pay a visit, she saw Noah leaning against the south barn wall, head bent over what she knew must be a letter from his great love, the blood Hank had said was still beating through his veins. Over the years since Virgil's death, Zorrie had often thought of that night when she had stood outside his room, speaking to him through the door, of the light that had poured out when it came open. Watching him work his eyes hard over the piece of near-crumpled paper in his hands, knowing he could not without this great labor make the words reveal their secrets to him, thinking of all the other letters it stood for and with, she turned quietly around.

She went home. She peeled more potatoes than she could have eaten in a week. She gulped at a tall glass of water. Some of it spilled out the corners of her mouth and slid down the sides of her chin and landed on the faded front of her yellow dress and felt cool there. She touched at the spots with her thumb and index finger and wondered if water spilling out of the corners of your mouth was a kind of weeping. When she and Harold were first married, she had knocked over a glass of something. The wet line had run off the table and fast down the waxed cloth and onto the floor, and Harold had said, "You've made the table cry," and she had said, "It's tears of joy," and Harold had said, "Then they must be mine, Mrs. Underwood." He had smiled then, such a smile, a smile to light the room, the day, the world entire, forever and ever, amen. She tried to lift the corners of her own mouth, but the tears there that were not tears but just water from the tall glass stopped her.

The phone rang. She stood feeling at the cool spots on her dress for as many rings as she could bear before she crossed the room and picked it up. Even after she cleared her throat, her voice wasn't ready to be used yet, so she waited there silently with the receiver pressed hard against her ear. The light crackling on the line seemed a language, like the wet in the corners of her mouth, that she might understand if she could only learn to listen harder. By and by the crackling gave up on her and coalesced into a voice that sounded like it was calling up from under a bridge or the bottom of a well. "Hello? Hello is that you, Ghost Girl?" the voice said.

IT TOOK ZORRIE so little time—barely more than a few hours, and no getting turned around—to reach Ottawa that after she had passed its outskirts, it seemed as though it wasn't just the miles but the decades that had been gobbled up by her Ford and that she should head for the abandoned barn and get ready to start thinking about sleeping on old straw and how she would best present herself for a job she desperately needed but knew nothing about. *That none of them had really known anything about.* This is what she thought when, the late afternoon of the day after the phone had rung, she stood beside Marie in front of Janie's grave in the Saint Columba Cemetery. The light gray stone had been planted in the earth so recently that, although Janie had been put into the ground nearly a year before, it still wore a dark collar of ruffled earth. Marie, who had detailed the difficult circumstances of Janie's death on the phone, now told Zorrie about the graveside service and the large group of brothers and sisters and nieces and nephews and children and friends who had gathered to say their fare-wells, and about the warm rain that had drizzled down like sweet syrup while the minister spoke, and the rainbow that had arisen as they were all walking back to their cars. She said that because of how bad things had been for Janie at the end, there had been no viewing, but it had been a pretty white coffin, the one in which she was now sleeping below their feet, just about as pretty as Janie had been when Zorrie had known her now long ago. Marie put her hand on the crenellated top of Janie's marker and closed her eyes a minute, then opened them and pointed out across the cemetery in the direction of the graves of the other girls whose bones were now glowing beneath the earth. It was said that the Luna powder stopped its shimmering after a while, but Marie didn't fully believe it.

"Maybe up here we stop seeing it, but not down there, down there they're all still lit up," she said.

They drove then to a café near the courthouse and sipped watery coffee and picked at slices of rhubarb pie as they filled each other in about some of the bend and twist of their lives. Marie said they had often worried that Zorrie wouldn't be able to find her way, that even her beloved Indiana wouldn't help her climb up out of the hurt that anyone with eyes could see had had a hold on her back then.

"Truth is, I did more of the worrying," she said, tapping with her fork at the side of her cup. "Janie said she thought you'd make it through. That you'd keep finding things worth finding. And look at you, driving your own truck and running your own farm. You've had a life. How right she was."

Before Zorrie could protest, could tell her about standing with water spilling out of her mouth by the kitchen sink when the phone had rung, Marie gave out a laugh that brought back memories and said she'd had herself a man, one of those nice-looking ones who had always been mooning around in the old days, but he hadn't ever been better than half a husband or a quarter of a father and had left the picture long ago. Janie had done a bit better in the man department, but not much. A tear bloomed up in the corner of Marie's eye when she said this. She must have felt it slide sidewise and down one of the wrinkles the decades had branded her with because she reached up and stopped it just before it looked set to skid down the line of her cheekbone. She said she hoped whoever had invented tears had taken out a patent, because there was big money in them.

"What do you think? Would you invest in a tear company?"

"I'm already a principal shareholder."

"You and me both, Ghost Girl. You and me both."

Marie then took a bite of her pie and a drink of her coffee and told Zorrie about how Janie had thought for a long time that she was in the clear, only for the aches in her jaw and neck and then in her extremities—ones that so many of the other girls had experienced—to set in. They had taken first one of Janie's legs and then the other. The treatments they inflicted on her had robbed her of her hair, which had been so thick and still brown, and seeing it go first by the strand and then by the clump had been one of the hardest things for both of them.

Despite Janie's voluminous family, which had never stopped growing, it had been Marie who Janie had most wanted with her at the end. Although they had quarreled when more and more girls at the plant started getting sick and Marie gave her notice but Janie would not, they had later reconciled and become better friends than ever. They had stayed as close as sisters over the years, had practically raised their children together, and often joked that they ought to have married each other and not the feckless husbands who had ultimately had such small parts to play in their lives.

"She talked about you, Ghost Girl," Marie said after a young waitress with a limp that seemed somehow a part of their conversation had poured them out more coffee. "She had about a thousand friends, but there toward the end your name came up more than once. You know she kept that pearl you found for her? I lost my shell many a year ago, but she always had that pearl. It sits now over yonder in a box at her oldest daughter's house. We both of us wondered what you had gotten up to, what curveballs you'd been thrown, which ones you'd swung at and missed. Which ones you'd hit. I said she didn't worry about whether you'd made it, but she did worry some that maybe you'd got yourself touched by the paint too, and though I told her you hadn't been there long enough to get into any trouble worth mentioning, we both said we ought to track you down and make sure. We always had it in mind to pick up the phone, since there couldn't be too many Zorries in the phone book out your way, or any way for that matter, but it kept not getting done, and then things got so bad. I'm only just now catching up."

Marie stopped and looked at Zorrie, her head cocked to one side. Zorrie realized that a question had been put to her, and thought she better try and answer it, but when she opened her mouth, nothing emerged. Marie waited a while and then shrugged and said, "Well, you're still here breathing God's good air, and so am I. For a little longer anyway."

At this Zorrie's eyes came up quickly from the coffee she had been stirring and studying, in hopes perhaps of finding in it some way to speak about Harold and fish hooks. Marie said that, yes, the cancer, close kin to the one that had ruined

Janie and so many of the other girls, had now made its mark on her dance card too, and that she would be starting treatment soon. Her own prognosis was generally positive, but she had seen up close what kind of a weapon it was she now had aimed at her and was feeling motivated to get things done. Sitting there with Zorrie, their good friend of a minute from the old days, was one of those things. She cried, and Zorrie took her hand and cried along with her, then after a while reached in her purse and brought out the card Janie had sent her.

"I remember that," Marie said, wiping at her face and nose and laughing a little out of embarrassment.

"She sent it to me must have been six or seven years back."

Marie took the card, turned it over, squinted, shook her head. "You could get whiplash trying to watch time go by. Did you sign up for that? I know I never did. Time'll spin your salad for you. My lord, yes it will. She finally got herself up there. She did indeed. Didn't stop talking about it for a week."

"I thought about trying it out myself."

"Did you?"

Zorrie said it hadn't happened, that she'd gotten stuck in sand. Marie said she knew what that was like. Said it didn't need to be quicksand to pull you in. As they took a turn through the old downtown, past the soda shop that was now a laundromat, and the old cinema where they had once seen Marlene Dietrich all lit up on the big screen in her silky gowns, then the plant where they had sucked on candy and painted their clock faces and pointed their brushes and blown kisses at their future doom, Marie said she wanted Zorrie to

understand that talk of tear patents and quicksand notwith-
standing, both she and Janie had lived good, happy lives. They
had talked on this a great deal.

"I wasn't there for the very last minutes, but Janie's brother
told me she went to her grace with a smile on her lips, and I
believe it too. She said she'd ridden shotgun to joy in too many
of life's roadsters to get mournful about it at the end. You were
a happy memory for her, Ghost Girl. For both of us."

Zorrie put the card on the dashboard where she could see
it and looked at it frequently the next morning on the drive
home. In saying her farewells to Marie, she had asked if there
was anything she could do to help her in what she now had
to face, and Marie had answered that Zorrie had already done
it just by making the drive and standing with her at Janie's
grave and remembering them both and listening to her rattle
on. She had her grown children for the hard days, and Janie's
family would not forget her either. As Zorrie put the key in
the ignition, Marie asked her, again and more directly this
time, if Zorrie was all right, and this time she found the words
to shape a reply. Although Marie had reassured her that a few
swallows of the Luna powder she and Janie and so many
others, unlike her, had gobbled practically by the barrelful for
years would not have hurt a baby, and that babies were just
sometimes lost, Zorrie could not help wondering if the beautiful powder had in fact found a way to wound her too.

Might it also have been that glow, she wondered as she
drove, the glow they had worn on their hands and faces and
clothes, that had robbed her of Harold? Had that glow stolen
her child, kept another from taking root, and somehow
grabbed up her husband too? Had he been looking at a

luminous clock face on the plane that had carried him down to the water? Had the walls of her insides been set to light by the powder she had drunk, when all within should have been warm and quiet and dark? Had that glow stolen Hank and Bessie? Had it reached back in time, taken her parents, and replaced them with her aunt? Had it seeped out the windows and across the fields to the Summerses' house and stolen Virgil's wits from him? Had it hurt Opal? Noah? *Poor dear Janie*, she thought. *Poor dear Marie. Poor all of us.*

She worked herself up enough that she had to pull over outside Remington and get out and walk around. She had just sunk her heel into some ditch mud and stepped partially out of her brown shoe when a turquoise coupe with its radio blaring went by. It honked. Zorrie waved. She knew she had heard the song before. She thought it must be Elvis Presley or Buddy Holly. She couldn't keep them straight, although she knew that one of them was dead. The car swerved one way and then the other, like it was dancing for her, and then it honked again and sped straight on. As she watched it vanish, she smiled. For there, just down the road from Ottawa, it was— Janie's roadster, a turquoise car made to dance for her across the concrete. And whether at the wheel it was joy or some of that old hope her aunt had so hated, it made her want to move her feet. To wave her hands. Right there on the road, she did both these things. Never mind that they made her blush. She whistled and hummed snatches of different songs she had heard and felt so calm by the time she got home that it did not seem strange to her that rather than taking the old tin of powder straight out into the backyard to bury it and set the dark world of the worms aglow, as she had intended when she first drove out of Ottawa, she simply moved aside the cigar box to uncover the copy of Virgil's Montaigne that she kept under it, tucked the card from Janie back into the yellowed pages, and, humming and grinning, closed it all up.

A QUICK INSPECTION of the old Victrola she and Harold had sometimes propped open to play scratchy songs by singers she couldn't remember confirmed that it was beyond repair, so she bought herself a new record player. The man who sold it to her said he would throw in some LPs, but when he started pulling out Beethoven and Bach, she said it wasn't funeral music she was looking for—what she had in mind was what they played at drive-ins and on the radio.

"Ah," said the man. "You're looking for the King."

The machine was bright red and portable and had a built-in speaker that was loud enough, when Zorrie turned the volume all the way up, to make her teeth rattle. She listened to Elvis Presley in the kitchen, Pat Boone in the living room, the Beach Boys in the basement, and the Chordettes in her bedroom. When she wasn't listening, she was often whistling. She wished Gus could hear her on "Mr. Sandman" or "Hound Dog," as she thought her technique was much improved. She rarely tapped her feet or swayed her shoulders when she had the music on, but she sang along to some of the songs and snapped her fingers frequently.

She was not, though, able to fully recapture the feeling she had had on the road back from Ottawa, and no matter how loudly she played Pat Boone or Buddy Holly, Janie and Marie and the whole lost world they represented kept swirling around her. It was a chance remark by Ruby, made while she was helping her hang laundry, that gave shape to her scattered thoughts about the two women. Zorrie had been humming what she only later realized was "That'll Be the Day" when Ruby said, "Noah's Opal used to hum like that while she hung." There wasn't any more to it, and when they were finished, Zorrie went home, but that comment followed by some thinking about the friendship Janie and Marie had built and made last across so many years, even unto death, all the while reaching out their hands to others, like her, which was surely a kind of love, an important one, was what she would credit with her decision to take a drive one rainy afternoon a few days later in the direction of Logansport. And while she did not on that first occasion go so far as to turn in when she came to the sign for the state hospital, she did slow down and peer out the window up the hill to the scattering of rain-dark buildings, in one of which Noah's great love, his Opal, passed her nights and days, and imagine what it might be like to call on her, say a kind word, and reach out her hand. That might have been it, just that one look and the thoughts and feelings that went with it, but two weeks later, after she realized that she wasn't much turning on her record player anymore, and that her foot tapping, if not her whistling and humming, felt like it had run its course and the gift of music might now better serve someone else, she got in her truck and drove over again.

Lester had that morning told her about a blueberry farm outside Logansport that his wife, Emma, had visited the previous weekend, so Zorrie stopped there on the way. It was a bright day, and the rows smelled earthy and sweet. Some of the berries had split and others had clearly been bird-pecked, but there were many more that were smooth, shiny, and whole. Zorrie picked with her right hand until it got tired, then switched to her left. The tips of her thumbs and forefingers grew sticky, and although she didn't eat many as she picked, as others around her clearly were, she did every now and again bring one quickly up to her lips. She filled a bucket and a small basket she'd lined with red-checked plastic and, carrying this latter in one hand and her record player in the other, walked through long, freshly painted halls behind a young nurse with a kind smile to the West Ward of the Logansport State Hospital and Opal's bed.

"You got yourself a visitor, honey, and she's got something exciting for you," the young nurse said, helping her to sit up and fussing with her pillows. She turned to Zorrie and said, "She's had a spell or two recently and is having some new treatments to help, so she might be feeling a little wore down."

"I'm not sleepy, Maggie," Opal said, fixing her eyes first on the nurse and then on Zorrie. Her eyes were a darker blue than Zorrie had ever seen in a face, as dark as the ripe berries she had brought, and they didn't seem to blink.

"That's fine, honey," the nurse said. "This is Zorrie Underwood. She's from over near where you lived in Clinton County before you came to us here. She brought you blueberries and a record player and wants to visit. I'll be back in a few minutes. You two enjoy yourselves."

The nurse walked over to a bed on the other side of the room, whose occupant appeared to be completely covered by a gray blanket. Whoever it was began to shake when the nurse came close and bent over her.

Opal looked at the basket of blueberries, then back up at Zorrie.

"I'm Opal," she said.

"Pleased to know you. I live on the farm next door to the Summerses," Zorrie said. "I've been there for a long while now. A good long while."

"Is that the record player you have brought me?"

"It is. Your nurse says you'll have to have permission to use it. Do you think you would enjoy having it? If they say you can use it?"

Opal brought a hand slowly up to the side of her face, pressed it firmly against her cheek, shut her eyes, and didn't open them for so long that Zorrie started to think her visit might be over before it had gotten started. Which, it struck her, might not be the worst thing. The night before, as she had lain in her own bed, with her own eyes closed, she had said to herself, more than once, "I just want to see her. I just want to do a kind thing." Now, standing here by a practically brand-new record player she wasn't entirely sure why she was giving away, with a basket of blueberries in her hand, in front of a woman who had been hospitalized for longer than Zorrie had lived on her farm, in a facility that had once been called the Northern Indiana Hospital for the Insane, in which patients quivered under gray blankets or shuffled in the halls, "I just want to do a kind thing" did not seem like much. And she'd had her look.

She stepped over, set the blueberries on a table by Opal's bed next to box of tissues, and turned to go. As she did so, Opal spoke.

"I'm not sleepy, Zorrie Underwood. I just got my eyes shut because of the colors. I'm grateful for the gift. I like music, and the doctor is an accommodating man. On Friday afternoons is when I'll play it. Please sit down."

There was a worn-out-looking wooden folding chair leaning against a radiator behind the table. Zorrie pulled it out, unfolded it, and set it up near Opal's bed. She put her purse in her lap, crossed her ankles, and said, "Thank you."

"When you shut your eyes, you're in a cave all your own making," Opal said.

Zorrie looked at Opal, shut her eyes, thought about caves, then opened them. Opal was looking at her again with the same unblinking stare as before. Zorrie wondered if during her time at the hospital she had taught herself to take all her blinks at once, maybe late at night, when the halls were empty and she was surrounded by the moans and murmurs of her fellows.

"Do you like blueberries?" Zorrie asked.

"Almost as much as I like music," Opal said. She spoke warmly in a voice that had retained much of what must once have been a great freshness, but her eyes did not blink and she did not smile. Her face, which had clearly once been terribly handsome, had lines in it that made Marie's and her own seem baby smooth, and she had an angry rash on her forehead. There was something off about her mouth. Zorrie suspected they had given her false teeth.

"You sure do have pretty eyes," Zorrie said.

"Pretty like the bright blue skies are these eyes, Zorrie Underwood."

"That's exactly right."

"Yes, it is."

"I'm friendly with Ruby and was with Virgil before he passed. It was my husband Harold's place before the war. You must have met him."

Opal looked at her. Poetry or no poetry about skies, it looked like she had blueberries in her eye sockets instead of pupils.

"My Harold got shot down in Holland during the war. I took over the farm. It isn't much, but I expanded some and have a good man to help run it. He's been around the area awhile. You might have known him too. Lester Dunn. He does most of the running lately, to tell the truth. Most of what I've been doing's running around."

Zorrie bit at the inside of her lower lip, uncrossed her ankles, and recrossed them.

"Noah's told me about you. He used to work with Harold sometimes. He likes your letters. It's about the only thing he likes in this world, as far as I can tell. He showed me one once about a whirlwind. They always said around home that you were about the sharpest pin in the cushion. Harold said you were as smart as a principal."

"I'd like to be buried in a dirt mound," Opal said.

Zorrie bit her lower lip again.

"They bury all kinds of things in there. That's where you can find pottery and oyster shells. Child toys too, nice ones with jeweled beads. There are also quite a number of sundry charred articles, each wearing its own black coat. It would be warm and quiet in a dirt mound. You could lie there a long time. The snow could fall and cover the whole wide world and there you would lie."

"I like that," said Zorrie.

" 'Out of this sun, into this shadow,' " said Opal.

"That's pretty. Is that something you thought up?"

"Well, Zorrie Underwood, that's more or less by an author. You will not find it in the Bible. It's not in any devotional.

I used to like to say it the other way around, 'Out of this shadow, into this sun,' but that is not the way the author wrote it down. It's harder the way she wrote it, but prettier and more true. Sometimes I get under my blanket and pretend that's where I already am. Under the ground, I mean. I told Phoebe Nelson what I do sometimes, and now she does it all the time. Maybe now on Friday afternoons we can do it with your music."

"Wouldn't that be too noisy?"

"Oh, no, we would play it soft."

Zorrie looked over at the bed with the gray blanket and imagined what it would be like to have warm dirt piled on top of her. No coffin, just dirt. Warm and soft. The King crooning quietly while she melted away.

"I had a friend they put into a coffin not too long ago. But it was a nice one, I'm told. All fresh and white. I've got another friend who might be going there soon," Zorrie said.

"I'm sorry to hear that."

"They were ghost girls. Over in Ottawa, Illinois. I guess I was one for a while too."

"Ghost girls, Zorrie Underwood?"

"Because after work we would glow in dark places like movie theaters."

"Or like in my cave!"

"Yes, just like that."

"Why, that's a beautiful thing."

"Yes, it was. While it lasted. For a short while. A long time ago."

"Don't you glow anymore?"

"Not in many a year."

"Maybe I'm a ghost girl, then, too."

"Maybe you are."

Zorrie then told Opal about Ottawa and the Radium Dial Company and her days with Janie and Janie's family and Marie. She told her about how even if the paint they had worked with eventually stopped glowing, it remained hot, and some of what had gotten inside you slithered into your bones and stayed there and never left even after you yourself had. She told Opal that she had swallowed spoonfuls of the paint when she was pregnant, and now feared she had hurt her own baby and did not know what she might have done to herself. She thought Opal, who had sucked in her breath like she wanted to speak, might offer some opinion or thought on all this, but instead she said, "They used to let me milk the cows in the dairy."

"Don't they anymore?"

Opal shook her head, shrugged, and let her hands flop in her lap.

"They tell me I am not doing well. They have obliged me to cut back on some of my customary pastimes. I have detailed everything to do with it in letters to my husband. It is distressing to us all, and I expect him to file a complaint."

Opal paused a moment, leaned forward, then said, "But do you know what the truth is, Zorrie Underwood?"

Zorrie shook her head.

"They are correct in their diagnosis. I am undeniably not all in all respects that I could be. It is correct that I be administered to. It is correct that visits from my husband are counterindicated. The doctor is both accommodating and just. It is appropriate that I should roll heavy balls and swallow chalky tablets and grasp after fruit that always escapes my hands. I have explained this to my husband too."

"Have you?"

"Yes, I have."

"He spends all his time thinking about you. Has done all these years."

Opal's face seemed to freeze, as if a coating of ice had suddenly settled on it. Then her dark pink tongue curled out, touched at something under her nose, stayed there a moment, then went slowly back into her mouth.

"Apart from the new rules and procedures, do they treat you well?" Zorrie asked.

"Oh, yes, Zorrie Underwood. We watch television. And we play games. And now we will listen to the records you have brought me on that shiny red record player. In addition, they let us hang out feeders for the hummingbirds. My, Zorrie, I do enjoy the sight of a little hummingbird."

At this, Opal, whose eyes had not once left Zorrie's, broke into a quick, tight-lipped smile that threw a pretty light up into her eyes but was gone almost as quickly as it had arrived. A moment later, she put her hand back up to the side of her face, turned her head, and looked out the window. Oaks and maples shivered slightly in a breeze. Two sparrows and a cardinal flicked by. Zorrie could still see the cardinal's red— which was almost a perfect match for the record player's— when she looked back at Opal. She could still see it a few minutes later when she stood to leave.

"It was sure nice to finally meet you, Opal," Zorrie said.

Opal, who had again shut her eyes, waved with her free hand and said, "It's a cave all your own, Zorrie Underwood.

Whether you glow in it or you don't. It's a cave behind your face. It's yours. It belongs to you."

ZORRIE THOUGHT ABOUT caves and shadows and blueberry eyeballs so much that evening that she did not sleep well and had nightmares she remembered when she woke up. She tried to chase them away by turning on the radio she had bought on her way home when she started to worry that she might after all miss being able to play something, but all she pulled in was static and she turned it off. For some time she'd had Oats in the house with her at night, and in the morning, as she sipped coffee and nibbled on toast, she told her about her dreams, about how she'd seen Oats running over soft earth that seemed to want her to stop and settle, and about how she had been back in the blueberry patch but couldn't pick anything because the bushes were alive and screamed if you touched them.

"What do you think of that?" she asked Oats.

Oats lifted her ears and made a noncommittal squeaking sound.

Zorrie got Oats her breakfast, then took the rest of the blueberries she'd picked over to Ruby, who thanked her and said she'd make a pudding and freeze the rest. She asked Zorrie what she planned to do with hers, and Zorrie said she didn't know, then said that in fact she hadn't got any for herself, that she'd picked them all to give away.

Ruby looked at her out of the corner of her eye, then said, "Well, Noah did say you've been acting strange."

"I went up to Logansport," Zorrie said.

Ruby either wasn't surprised or didn't act it. "How is she?" she asked.

"I don't know," said Zorrie. "I didn't know how to tell."

"I never knew either most of the time." Ruby took a berry out of the bucket, rolled it back and forth between her thumb and index finger, then popped it into her mouth. She sighed and said, "That's been a lifetime ago, and here it still is."

"She talked a fair amount about caves. She said she wanted to be buried in a dirt mound like the Indians."

"That was always her kind of talk. Virgil enjoyed it immensely. Said she was someone he could converse with. Of course Noah did too. Enjoy it, I mean."

"I gave her my record player. I wasn't using it anymore. I don't even know why I bought it in the first place."

"I bet she'll like that."

"You think they'll let her use it?"

"I don't know."

"Should I tell him? About going up there."

"Noah?"

Zorrie nodded.

Ruby picked out another blueberry and put it in her mouth. She chewed once or twice and then swallowed.

"He already knows you went up there. He told me yesterday you were going to."

"Sometimes I just know things. I expect we all do, even if we most of us don't pay it any mind," Noah said when Zorrie saw him next. She had been cultivating in the west field and spotted him working out in his beans with a hoe. When Zorrie came over, he had thanked her for the blueberries and said he hoped she had enjoyed meeting his wife. She said she had. That she had hoped they could be friends. Noah said he imagined the experience of meeting Opal had thrown her some. Zorrie said it had a little at first, but then she had settled into it and had found Opal about as bright and pleasant as could be. Noah said that was nice to hear. He said it had been kind of Zorrie to make the trip, and he could understand her curiosity. Zorrie had known about Opal for a long time, and it made sense that she would want to go up and see her. Especially since she really wasn't all that far away. That the distance had to do with cornfields and strips of dirt, not oceans. That oceans had nothing to do with it except in Noah's head. In his head the distance grew ever greater with the years and not smaller, as he had once thought it might, and try as he might, he hadn't figured out how to see his way to the other side. He had thought that one day time would have so salved the wound that he would almost be able to step out of his front door and straight in through the gates of Logansport. He had gone to see Opal once, soon after she had been taken, and his arrival and request for admittance had so upset her that he had promised to abide by her doctor's advice and the restrictions her family had put in place and wait to return. Somehow he was waiting still. Time wasn't doing what he had thought it would, what he thought, in truth, it had promised to. He smiled as he spoke, his smile bigger than Zorrie was used to seeing on his face, and it made her think of Opal's own tiny smile and of her mouth with something off about it. Noah spoke, smiling all the time, his voice increasing in speed and volume, his smile growing farther and farther away from something meant to indicate pleasure, and Zorrie, who already was not feeling altogether settled about her visit, began to feel certain she'd made a mistake. When he paused, she started to explain that it had been about her old sick friend and glow-in-the-dark paint and being lonely, so lonely, and wanting to do something, offer some gift, but trailed off when she realized that all of that, even the loneliness, was only the smaller portion of why she had gone. They stood a moment, looking at each other, and then Noah spoke, his voice calm again.

"Thank you for the blueberries, Zorrie. And thank you for taking some to Opal. She always liked them."

THAT FALL SAW the first in a series of uncommonly good harvests, which after several years had much of the community feeling more comfortable than they had in quite some time. Lester, who had started saving long before, used his share of the profits to buy a small farm near Boyleston that a cousin had put up for sale. Zorrie drove over with him one November morning and agreed that it was fine acreage. She gave him some of her tools and, since she had invested in a new machine the previous spring, let him buy her old tractor for next to nothing. He would still help her out, but now he'd have land of his own.

Lester and Emma sold their house in Hillisburg and moved out to their farm the first week of December. Around Christmas they had a party, and everyone agreed they'd done a good job sprucing the old place up. Zorrie helped string popcorn, ate a fair amount of it, cracked a few nuts, and sat by the fire. She had spoken to Marie the morning before and was feeling pleased about how well she had sounded despite the treatment she was undergoing, which had robbed her of her hair too. "Least they haven't taken any of my ambulatory instruments!" Marie had said, and they both laughed. It felt good to laugh about something that wasn't funny. Not funny at all. Emma had eggnog in a punch bowl on the sideboard, and the whole house smelled of nutmeg and good home-skimmed cream.

Candy Wilson sat and visited with Zorrie for a stretch. She'd had back surgery over the summer and still wasn't comfortable sitting without the special pillow she'd left at home. She also hadn't gotten used to the idea of cutting down and couldn't resist eating more than her share of the heavily iced angel cookies Phyllis Dunn had brought. There was a pair of girls chasing up and down the stairs, and after a time Emma called them over for a present. Zorrie watched them tear their way into a pair of matching harmonicas, which, upon the instructions of some adult Zorrie couldn't see, they walked around the room showing to all who had come. There was something about the half-jaunty, half-shy way they went around the room, holding up their instruments and making breathy first attempts at blowing through them, that reminded Zorrie of her own long-ago Christmases.

Her aunt had been wildly deficient as a maternal substitute, but she had never missed out celebrating Christmas. Zorrie always had a stocking filled with fruit, nuts, and maybe a top or a whistle waiting for her when she woke the morning of the twenty-fifth. Sometimes there had even been a tree, hung with glass balls and garlanded with popcorn and tinsel, and when she was small Zorrie had enjoyed nothing more, when her aunt wasn't around, than lying on the floor beneath it and gazing up through its fragrant boughs. Once, when her aunt had come in unexpectedly and caught her at it, she had surprised Zorrie more than she had ever been surprised in her life by lying right down next to her. After they had both lain there unspeaking under the tree for some good while her aunt had surprised her even more by saying, "I can see why you do this. It's peaceful and it's pretty." As the little girls sped giggling and already blowing credible scales past Zorrie, who refrained from importuning them any more than by smiling and nodding, her thoughts turned from the rare good memory of her aunt to Mr. Thomas. Mr. Thomas had also been an avowed enthusiast of Christmas, and more than once on snowy December days before the winter break, he had told stories about what he called German Christmas. In German Christmas, Santa Claus wore green trimmed with pure gold instead of red with white fur and had wings so he didn't need any reindeer to help him fly around the world. In German Christmas everyone got the same number of presents, and it didn't matter how you'd behaved as long as you hadn't robbed any banks or killed anyone.

When Noah sat down next to Zorrie, after the girls had been released to go back to racing up and down the stairs, she said, "Have you ever heard about how they used to do Christmas over in Germany? My old teacher in school liked to tell us about it. He went down to Evansville and, far as I know at least, never came back, and I have always been sorry about that."

Noah didn't respond. He sat with one hand on each of his knees, his back straight, his eyes looking out over the room.

"Did you get some eggnog?" Zorrie asked.

"Ruby is sick," Noah said.

Zorrie's smile slid off her face and fell into her lap. She swallowed hard and looked over at him. Just then Reverend

Carter came by. He had lately taken to coughing quite a bit and had lost a good deal of weight. When asked about it, he would only spread his hands, palms upward, shrug, and look at the sky. He was drinking coffee that wasn't just coffee. He nodded briefly at Noah but engaged Zorrie, so it was some time before she could ask, "How sick?"

"Well, Zorrie, if there was an Oats to it, she more than likely wouldn't come visiting much longer."

Zorrie walked down first thing the next morning with a bouquet of dried roses, zinnias, and chrysanthemums. Noah gave her a big blue mason jar to put them in, and she followed him upstairs. Ruby's color wasn't good, and the whites of her eyes looked gray. She was lying under three blankets and had a hot water bottle on her stomach.

"It's for my hands," she said. "I can't keep them warm. Noah fills it for me. Holds them too sometimes. Thank you for the flowers. You don't get a nice dried bouquet anymore."

Noah pointed at a red armchair pulled up next to the bed. Zorrie sat and asked Ruby if she was comfortable. Ruby said she was not, but that her discomfort had nothing to do with her cold hands or the quality of the care she was receiving.

They sat without speaking, the morning light spilling a shaft through the east window that was filled with slowly whirling dust motes, a good kind of glow. Some of the warm, dust-filled light fell across Ruby's legs, and Zorrie was tempted to reach her hand out to it. She said as much, and Ruby told her to go on, said the light was pretty this morning and she'd had the same thought more than once.

Zorrie looked at Ruby. "If we helped, could you lean forward?"

Ruby narrowed her eyes and smiled. She looked at Noah, who nodded and took his hands out of his pockets. She said, "I suppose I'm not quite coffin-fill yet."

Zorrie and Noah put a hand each behind Ruby's back and, when she was ready, pressed softly forward as Ruby held out her arms, fingers outstretched, so that for a minute it looked like the rest of the room was submerged in dark and it was only that shimmering band of sun to interrupt the long night. Ruby held her hands up to the wrists for a long moment in the deep yellow light, then sighed and, with their help, leaned back again.

"Those were about the prettiest pair of hands I ever saw," Zorrie said.

"Thank you for that, Zorrie," Ruby said.

"Yes, thank you, Zorrie Underwood," Noah said.

Ruby passed in her bed on a sunny day in early January, "very gentle," as Noah put it. There was a viewing at Frye's in Frankfort, and everyone agreed she looked beautiful in her green suit and silver cross. Zorrie squeezed Noah's arm after she went past the coffin, then stood out in the snow as they lowered Ruby into the frozen earth the next day. Ruby's coffin was deep brown, not white, but it looked comfortable, and she hoped Ruby's rest beneath the earth would be as soothing as it had seemed to her, when she thought about it, Janie's must be. Noah held his arms fixed at his sides and couldn't keep his eyes off the hole as the minister spoke. There was a lunch in the church basement afterward. Noah ate nothing and kept looking out the window in the direction of the cemetery. At one point he stood up from the table, walked up the steps, stood outside in the snow for a time, then came back down, his eyes watery, his cheeks red. Zorrie wondered if word had been gotten to Opal and suppressed an urge to go over and sit by him. When people came forward to put their hand on his shoulder and speak, he listened with great attention and then pressed his lips together and nodded his head.

A deep silence fell over the Summerses' house after Ruby's death. Zorrie tried to stop by every day at first, but Noah often wasn't home and didn't always come to the door when she knew he was. On warmer days Zorrie took walks along the lane with Oats in hopes of spotting him out in the barnyard, but either her timing was off or he wasn't around. She pictured him, in his grief, sitting alone in the cold house under the painting of blue cornflowers. Her own dark times over the days and years flapped like witch moths before her eyes then, and the distance between her heart and Noah's seemed smaller. Grief seemed to constitute a kind of connective membrane, not a divide, and the "fragile film of the present" felt strengthened, not threatened, by the past. Tears, it struck her—even ones that spilled out of your mouth or off a table— formed a fretwork the wingless could learn to walk over, if there had been enough of them and you tried. She wondered if Noah had long since intuited something like this, that it was the very reason he had remained so close in feeling to Opal even when he had let the less than forty miles that separated them become something so large.

Zorrie mentioned none of this of course when she did see Noah, yanking up a fence post, working on his truck, buying groceries in town. Instead they spoke of the weather or the respective merits of whichever product one or the other of them was considering buying. Zorrie did not bring up Ruby, nor Virgil for that matter, and Noah mentioned neither of them. He seemed on these occasions to be calm and self-possessed, but Zorrie suspected that there was plenty going on in the "cave behind his eyes."

In fact, one afternoon in early May when Zorrie was out on the lane with Oats, she spotted Noah standing by his barn with his back to her. She was about to call out a greeting to him when she realized that his shoulders were curled, that he was shaking slightly and had his face in his hands. Zorrie was torn between rushing toward him and moving on. She moved on. When she saw him again, on her way back, he spotted her as he came out of the barn and waved and called out to Oats.

That night she sat up late with Oats snoring at her feet and thought about caves. She had spoken that afternoon to Marie, and though her old friend had sounded as cheerful as ever, and they had found more than one thing to laugh about, there had been a crack or two in Marie's voice that Zorrie had found troubling, as if some huge hole might open up under Marie and suck her in. Zorrie had recently watched a television program on the great caves in southern Indiana and Kentucky, their vaulted halls lit by electric lamps, their walls glittering with metals and minerals with beautiful names. There were underground rivers that ran through some of the caves, and passages you had to crawl through if you wished to visit them. These caves had been partially inhabited by the Indians—learning that had made Zorrie think even more than she had already been thinking about her visit to Logansport—and were cousins in a way to the caves in France that had been painted on tens of thousands of years before. Many of the chambers were strewn with the bones of animals and bore the remains of fires lit by hands dead five hundred years. When the electric lights were switched off, the caves with all their wonders went back to the darkness that was their natural state.

Zorrie tried to imagine what it would be like to have the lights switched off when you were miles from the entrance, for the world around you to go as dark as it was indecipherable. She closed her eyes and thought about the lights getting switched off when she was lost in thought in her own "cave." She kept them closed even when she started, ever so slightly, to panic. After a time, though, it seemed to her that the dim halls and passageways of her mind, which were lately always too loud and too hot, began to fill with soft, cool, silencing dirt. It occurred to her then that it was silence and not grief that connected them, that would keep them forever connected, the living and the dead—her, Noah, Opal, Harold, Janie, Marie, her parents, maybe the whole world, and that this was not such a bad thing, especially if every now and then there was a little Buddy Holly or June Carter Cash playing away off somewhere in the background.

V

Our hands touch, our bodies burst into fire

Zorrie woke at dawn and smelled smoke before she'd made it halfway down the stairs. Oats barked once when she got to the kitchen and ran straight for the back door. Zorrie stepped outside, saw red through the trees, heard sirens in the distance, and ran for her keys.

She arrived just after the fire trucks and made sure she pulled well off the driveway so any others could get by. There were two trucks, one from Kempton, one from Hillisburg, and an ambulance. When she saw its doors fly open, her breath went and her heart started hammering again, even though it had slowed when she saw it was Noah's barn, not his house, that was burning. One of the firemen ran over to the house and banged on the door with a gloved hand. Zorrie put her fist to her mouth, bit into it hard, started forward, then stopped when she started to feel faint. But then she heard a shout muffled by the snarled roar of the fire and saw Noah over by

Ruby's greenhouses, holding a bale of straw. His forearms were smeared with black, his nostrils flared, his eyes looked too large for his head. Oats, who had come across the woods, broke from the lane, skirted the barn, and dashed toward him, barking wildly. Noah lifted the bale over his head and flung it toward the blaze. It fell short but still burst into flame. The fireman who had been banging on the door made a signal to the EMTs and started for Noah. Zorrie put her fist back to her mouth and followed him.

Noah had inhaled smoke and couldn't stop coughing. He answered in the negative when asked if there was any livestock or explosive material in the barn, but refused to let himself be examined by the ambulance crew. Whenever they approached, he would flail his arms, fists bunched, and between fits of coughing yell that he was crazy, that they couldn't touch him unless they planned on taking him up to Logansport and locking him the hell away. One of them, Frank Wright's boy Jeff, put an arm on Noah's back and was hit so hard Zorrie heard him mention restraint and sedation to his partner. Oats had gone mostly quiet when Zorrie came over. She sat off to the side growling and whining and looking from the thick jets of water trained on the roof and backside of the barn, where the flames, fifteen feet high in places, were worst, to Noah, Zorrie, and the two calm but frustrated men.

Hank arrived just after a third fire truck had pulled up, took a quick survey of the scene, and pulled the medics aside. A moment later they went over to their ambulance and drove away. Zorrie, who had found herself unable to speak since she got close to Noah and saw the crazed look in his eyes, walked quickly over to Hank, leaned close, and said, "It might have been best if you'd have let them give him something. He's not right."

Hank looked at Noah, who was staring straight at him with his tongue partway out of his mouth, blackened fingers digging hard into his own arm. "I know it, Zorrie. But we got a mess here. It's the county pays their salaries, and even if they're good boys, under the circumstances I thought it best they vacate expeditiously."

The image of Noah coming out of the huge barn the night before and calling to Oats presented itself to her. She started to speak, but Hank was walking over to him.

"You goddamn tell them to come get me," Noah said, coughing and retching and looking more frightening to Zorrie in his rage and hurt and madness than the jets of dark orange fire rushing up out of the ruined wood. "You tell them it's goddamn time. I'm the one set this going and I'm the one that's crazy and they better come and goddamn get me and goddamn take me away *now*."

Hank walked straight up to Noah, slapped him, then took him by the shoulders and shook him hard. Noah kept coughing and telling him to send for the hospital, that he was crazy, that they had to come, he'd set his own fire now, he'd waited long enough. Hank just stood there, half circles of sweat blooming out under his shoulder blades. After a time Noah, who did not stop talking, seemed to grow calmer, but Hank kept his hands on his shoulders. He stood there staring into Noah's eyes, listening or not listening to everything Noah said, but either way not answering. He was still standing there when he told Zorrie, who had not moved either, that things were under control and she might just as well take Oats and go on home.

"I can't go," she said.

Hank said he wasn't asking.

As she pulled away, Oats scrabbling unhappily on the seat beside her, others arrived. Lester, who'd only stepped down from the Hillisburg volunteer fire department the year before, came up fast, parked in the side ditch, and jumped out of his truck. Some stayed in their cars. Candy Wilson sat at the wheel of her Lincoln, a fat hand over her mouth and upper lip, tears streaking her cheeks, large glasses reflecting bits of flame.

THE WIND SHIFTED midmorning, and what was left of the smoke moved out over the fields. The smell, though, stayed in the air, drifted in Zorrie's hallways, hung over the kitchen table, even came out of the cupboard when Zorrie opened it to get a bowl. With the wind changed, it would have been easy for Zorrie to look out her side windows, over the emerald rows of new corn, and see the fire engines pulling away from what must now be a sodden, smoldering pile, but she did not look. Instead she sat in her chair, flipped through the pages of an atlas Harold had once purchased for her, and played at seeing how many countries and cities she could recognize. When she tired of that, she thumbed through garden supply catalogs and debated whether to place an order for a new shovel with a patented rubber handle or just run into town and buy one. Once or twice she felt a twist in her stomach and wondered if Noah was still talking and Hank was still standing there, with his hands on Noah's shoulders, or if he had failed in absorbing all Noah had to say and Noah had gotten his wish, officials from the Logansport State Hospital coming to ferry him across the imaginary chasm to a bed down the hall from Opal's, where, with the endorsement of the medical community, he could slide down under his own covers and shiver out the rest of his days.

Lester stopped by that afternoon after he had gone home and showered. Zorrie brought out ice water and they stood under one of the hickories near the house. Lester said it had been about the worst barn fire he'd seen, and he'd seen some. The Summers barn, built by Ruby's grandfather, had either been the biggest or one of the biggest in the county and had been crammed to the rafters with things that hadn't been hesitant to burn. They'd salvaged a number of fine old tools and seen the sorry remains of just as many more. Lester said everyone over there knew the fire had been set, not least because Noah had kept up telling everyone who'd come up to him even after he'd quieted down that now, because of what he'd done, they'd have to take him away. Lester also said that Hank, who in addition to his peacekeeping duties was Johnson Township fire inspector, had said loud enough for everyone to hear, and with not a drop of humor in his voice, that even if it were a crime to set your own property on fire, which in this case it wasn't, it was clear that faulty wiring was to blame.

"He wanted them to take him to Opal," Zorrie said. "To help him do what he can't figure out how to get done on his own."

"That appears to be about the size of it," said Lester, taking a sip of water and licking his lips. He swished the water around in his mouth, breathed loudly in through his nose, and said he couldn't get rid of the smoke taste. Zorrie said she'd even tried gargling Listerine, that nothing had helped.

Lester grimaced, rubbed his index finger across his front teeth. "There's a piece of wall didn't get burned. Sticking up out that mess. They put their names on it."

"Who did?"

"They did. Says 'Noah and Opal Summers.' She must of wrote it."

"He can write."

"I've seen his writing. Kind of hard to read. This was neat and didn't look like it took a week to set down."

Zorrie tried to remember where she had been when Opal was living at the Summerses'. Was she still at her aunt's? Had Ottawa already come and gone? It bothered her that she couldn't immediately recall. She had been young, certainly. Young but heading toward her life. Heading toward Gus and Bessie and Harold with his green eyes and strong hands. Heading toward Noah and his sorrow and all these years now living on this farm alone.

Lester drained the remaining water in his glass, crunched an ice cube, and looked at her. "You all right, Zorrie? Hank said you were out there a while this morning. There's nothing simple about seeing a thing like that."

A jay landed on one of the hickory's lower branches. It took two quick steps sideways, pecked at its right wing, let out a screech, and flew off out of sight. Zorrie nodded. Nothing simple at all, she thought, seeing Hank holding Noah, Oats running wildly, the firemen hollering at each other, water pouring through the smoke and steam and flames.

Lester shoved a hand into his pocket, sucked another ice cube into his mouth, and shook his head. "He thinks you burn your barn down and jump around and they come and it just works that way. Everyone knows Noah has his troubles, but the variety of crazy where you go off forever isn't one of them."

Hank Dunn, who rolled up not long after Lester had left to see how Zorrie was coming in the wake of the morning's "grotesqueries," concurred. He said that even if Noah had some indisputable strange to him, there was still a great deal too much reason in his behavior to make anyone want to get the white jackets on the phone. What he had done was stupid and better than halfway criminal, but also had a logic to it if you gave it a close look. Opal's family didn't want him up in Logansport and had arranged things to make sure he stayed away, so he'd thought maybe now that Ruby wasn't around to upset, he could hurdle over that impediment by pulling out a matchbook of his own. But that was where the scenarios diverged. He hadn't sat down in the middle of the barn the way Opal had sat down in the middle of the house she had set on fire. They had both wanted their fires to take them away, but his was the only one in which, according to the plan, its igniter was supposed to end up alive.

"All right," said Zorrie. "But why he didn't years ago just go up there and sign her out and bring her home and find some way to take care of her here? Ruby would have helped. We all would. What does it matter what her family had to say about it? She's his wife."

Hank took off his hat and wiped at some of the grime and sweat he hadn't yet got fully cleaned off his brow. "But that's just it," he said after sucking in a deep breath. "That's the whole burnt biscuit, Zorrie. She *isn't*."

"Isn't what?"

"His wife."

"I don't follow."

"They were never married."

"They aren't married?"

"Not in the legal sense. And they weren't together anything like long enough for common law. When they met, Opal was an adult ward of her family—or I forget what the term was—had spent half her teenage years in that place where she's now lived out most of her life. All they had was an arrangement."

"You mean they were engaged?"

"They called it a trial run. Her family was just happy to have her kind of trouble off their hands, for good they hoped, and Virgil was forward-thinking and persuasive enough with his references to the unorthodox practices of the ancients, I suppose, that Ruby went along with it. I can't even remember why, beyond friendship, they told me. I wasn't but a deputy who liked to listen to Virgil talk back then. They reckoned they'd see if it made sense to get the preacher and the court-house involved at the end of a year."

"I'd forgotten it was less than a year."

"It was Virgil called Logansport—because if he hadn't, my office would have had to—when Noah just about didn't come back out of that house of theirs with her in his arms. Her family took the reins on keeping Noah away after that."

"And everyone knows this?"

"If everyone is me and now you, then everyone does. As far as folks around here were concerned, they got married right and proper over where she was from."

Whether by design or chance they had both turned away from the direction of the smoke and ruin and stood now facing south across the clear fields toward Indianapolis. Zorrie put the backs of her hands on her hips.

"Why, Hank?"

"Why did they think that?"

"No, why are you telling me this?"

Hank shrugged, cleared his throat, spat to the side, and then apologized for spitting. For a time he got interested in some smudge on the side of his shirt, and then he scratched a while at his bare forearm. When he spoke again, his voice came out quiet and slow.

"Because the way I see it, our friend down the road is about out of angels, Zorrie. He needs people who care about him more than a handshake on Sunday. People who'll stick around longer than the time it takes to slurp down a cup of coffee."

"Like you and me, you mean."

"Like *you* especially, is what I was thinking."

"I see."

Zorrie took in a breath through her nose and shifted her weight from one foot to the other. Her neck was sore, like she'd slept wrong on it, and her shirt felt stickier against her back than she liked. Oats, who wasn't over being agitated, went trotting across the yard and plunged with a bark into some rogue horseweed that had thus far escaped Zorrie's scythe. When Hank spoke again, he looked her in the eye.

"I hope it's all right that I'm speaking plain. When I brought up the subject before, back when I used to come calling, it was disappointment doing some of the talking. I won't deny that. It's the truth. This time it derives from necessity."

Zorrie kept her eyes locked on Hank's and put a hand to her cheek. She was pleased to note that she hadn't blushed. Thought maybe the heat of the morning's inferno had stolen off her own and hoped it was slow in coming back.

"We need to watch over him for a minute," Hank said. "We need to watch him close. He's going to get himself thrown in jail, not into a straitjacket, or just ruin himself if he pulls another trick like this one. I don't think he's got but the one fire in him, and I told him I believed that, this morning, somewhere up on a dozen times, but I don't know how well he heard me."

"You had just slapped him."

"And he had just burned his own barn down."

"So you want me to go down there and knock on his door and repeat the message? Tell him the one fire is all he gets?"

"Something like that," said Hank. "I don't know what would be best. I expect the first part of that equation would be enough."

ZORRIE WASN'T SO sure. Didn't know what just putting her knuckles on his door would accomplish. Couldn't imagine what her version of grabbing Noah hard and telling him he had to put away the matchbooks forever would look like. She did her best to make her mind fill up with the previous night's cool dirt, but the fact of the fire and the fact that Noah and Opal had never been officially married and the fact that her heart was hammering so loudly it was making her feel sick kept the soft, cool dirt from coalescing. She thought about it all too much to too little purpose for far too much of the night, and the next morning she got up early and made a pie. Somewhere after midnight, when she had come to the conclusion that arriving with the makings of a decent meal would be the least worst approach she could take, she had settled on using some of the cherries from the deep freeze, but in the morning light the red showing through the clear plastic looked too bright for the circumstances, so she pitted and chopped up white peaches, measured out sugar, flour, and cinnamon, stirred it all up, and poured it into her crust. Then she peeled and sliced potatoes, working carefully because she had cut herself twice in the past week, once fairly deeply. She liked the way the old blade moved through the tight, grainy texture of the potatoes, the settling whack it made on the board, the film of starchy moisture on the old, dark metal, on the tips of her fingers, on the knuckles of her sturdy hand. When she was finished, she set the slices in a glass dish, sprinkled salt and pepper on them, poured in some milk and dollops of lard, and covered the whole thing with shredded Colby cheese. Then she went out to the garden, cut off a head of lettuce, pulled some radishes and carrots, dug up a sweet onion, and, doing her best to ignore the smell of smoke that was still everywhere, picked two good-looking beefsteak tomatoes. She washed and sliced these things, set them next to the sink, then changed, took her keys, and ran into town.

When she got back, she put ground ham in a bowl, tore up some bread, cracked eggs, and mixed it all together. She spooned in salt, dried thyme, and garlic powder, put the mixture into a deep pan, and looked at the clock. When she had it all in the oven, she went upstairs to take a bath.

SHE HAD INTENDED to no more than glance at the remains of the barn, but when she pulled into Noah's driveway, the sight of the plumes of smoke still lifting bleakly up out of the charred black ruin drew her over in spite of her resolve. She stood at the edge of what the day before had been the big white doors and was now like the black border of a bad thought. At some point the back wall had given out, and part of the roof had fallen over and crushed what hadn't been burned of Noah's garden. A few smoke-blackened corn stalks had escaped the collapse and shivered a little, like there might still be some point to such efforts, in the sun and breeze. Much of the surroundings had been trampled. There were tire tracks everywhere and boot marks in the mud surrounding the ruin. The smell, which she had earlier just caught the edges of, was the worst. It made her think of being locked up and forgotten in an old coal cellar or in a similar place where hope was no longer and never again would be. She could see the part of the wall that had survived the fire, but one of the firemen or Noah had stacked some boards up against it and obscured the writing there.

Having knocked once, she stood outside Noah's side door no more than five seconds before he opened it. He did not seem at all surprised to see her and helped her get the food out of her truck and into the kitchen. He set the table while she unloaded the hot dishes, then the two of them sat down in the places they'd taken when she'd come down on Thursday nights. Zorrie had always liked sitting with a view out the big double windows, but now, finding herself looking out past the spirea, beyond the oaks, to an ugly corner of the burned barn, she wished she'd chosen another seat. Still, when Noah asked if maybe she wouldn't be more comfortable on the other side of the table, out of the sun, she thanked him but said she'd sit where she always had, if that was all right.

Noah took large helpings of everything, ate with appetite, and complimented the food. Zorrie nodded and ate lightly and stole glances at him, trying to decide if he looked different to her after what he had done, and after what she now knew. Really he just looked like a somewhat shinier version of his normal self. There was a decent bruise on his left cheek where Hank had hit him, but he had bathed and washed his hair and had on a clean gray shirt under his overalls. It looked like he had taken extra care with his hands. Yesterday they had been almost black from the wrists down, as if he had plunged them into a barrel of soot. Today, though, when he lifted his glass of lemonade, his rough fingernails glistened and the dark pink flesh of his scars picked up the overhead light.

After Noah had had a second slice of ham loaf, over which he'd drizzled a fair amount of the sauce that had collected in the bottom of the pan, Zorrie cleared the table and brought out a couple of Ruby's small plates for pie. When she asked Noah how big a piece she ought to cut for him, he didn't answer, just stared at the cabinets. She swallowed and asked again, and when still he didn't answer, she cut off a medium-sized slice, set it on a plate in front of him, scooped up the crust and chunks of caramelized peach that had stayed stubbornly behind, and set that on the plate too. Then she cut herself a small slice and took a drink of lemonade. She lifted her fork, brought it down through the crust, touched against the peach mixture inside and brought it up again, then set it down on the table when he started talking. While he talked, his eyes flashing, his nostrils slightly flared, she folded her hands in front of her and, as she had pictured herself doing all morning, looked straight at him without saying anything, like Hank had. When after several minutes he paused, she nodded, said, "All right," took up her fork, brought it down through the crust and peaches, lifted it to her mouth, and let her lips close. She chewed and nodded and then set her fork next to her plate and folded her hands again.

"That's fine pie if I do say it myself," she said.

Noah, who seemed to have sworn himself quiet for a minute, took a deep breath, looked at his plate, then off at the cabinets, then at his plate again. Zorrie leaned her head to the left and gazed out the window. There was a light breeze lifting the spirea and a few sweat bees hanging stubbornly in the air. She let her eyes sweep past the oak to the black ruin and then brought them to the spirea again. Then she took another bite and chewed. Noah lifted his fork and tapped at the pie. He started to say something but stopped and instead took a bite himself. He chewed and swallowed and took another bite and gave a compliment. Zorrie looked at him. He smiled and then started talking again.

When Hank called her that afternoon to see if she had paid her visit, she said she had, but that there hadn't been any angel wings involved in any of it. She had just listened to him swear until he was sworn out.

The next day she brought a fresh salad and fried chicken and heated up the leftover potatoes and pie. They sat as they had the day before, and dinner passed in much the same way, only this time Noah started in on his gesticulating and talking earlier in the proceedings and went on with it even longer. Like the day before, however, he did finish most of the large portions he served himself and didn't forget to compliment and thank her. Zorrie had decided it would be all right if she ate while she listened and managed to get through her meal while it was all still hot. The barn had stopped smoking, and when her eyes fell on its jagged contours at stray moments during the meal, she found it didn't bother her quite as much.

A good deal of what Noah said, she had heard him telling Hank the morning of the fire, the main difference now being that his remarks were tinged with what Zorrie took to be a mixture of outrage and disbelief that he had not, despite the gravity of his gesture, been taken away. Having heard him with Hank, Zorrie wasn't surprised when he discussed his "own folly and goddamn madness," but after a while his swearing began to wear on her, and on the third day that she made dinner for him, she used a break in his commentary to tell him she didn't know about his assertions and confessions about wrapping straw around a piece of wire and setting a match to it like only a madman would, but there was no call to use ill-colored words.

The next day, over roast flank steak and potatoes, he apologized to her for his language and thanked her for getting his dinner and listening to him.

"You go on and keep making speeches all you want if you think it'll help you get through this patch," she said.

"I wish it was just a patch, Zorrie," he said.

"You'll get through it, Noah Summers. I know you will."

Hank checked in and seemed satisfied by the direction of things. He had driven by several times at night and twice in the early morning before sunrise and each time found everything quiet, the world of the Summers farm soft and still. Neighbors stopped by while she was there, but they didn't stay longer than was required to, yes, drink a cup of coffee and, some of them, shake Noah's hand. No one seemed to think it was strange that Zorrie was sitting in Noah's kitchen in the middle of the day or working on his dishes. At church, Candy Wilson said it was good of Zorrie to have taken such an interest in Noah, that she would have done the same if she'd been as close to Ruby and Virgil as Zorrie had. Ralph Duff agreed. He said Noah needed company and human talk and good things on his table to set him right. After he'd lost Helen, his girls had prayed with him and made sure he kept his head above water, made sure he had what he needed so he didn't drown.

"What do you two talk about?" Ernest Johnson asked.

"This and that," Zorrie said.

Reverend Carter, who had lately begun to look permanently green around the gills and had more than a little trouble getting his voice to the back of the room when he was preaching, said she was acting in a Christian way and suggested she bring Noah along with her when she came next week. Zorrie said she would put the question to him if it seemed right, and Reverend Carter said that question was always right. The reverend had started to smell sour, like old clothes or silage that hadn't settled. Zorrie had never liked how close he leaned when he talked, how the sharp movements of his hands seemed to form a barrier around a body that was difficult to break away from, but she told him she would see if it was something that seemed appropriate to bring up.

She hurried home after church to heat up the green beans and ham she'd cooked that morning in the pressure cooker and slice up some cucumbers and onions. It was an unusually fresh day, with fine breezes and a warbler stringing its bright song across the yard. The light coming in through the window glazed the zinnias she'd brought over and set in the center of the table, reminding her of Ruby and that day in the bedroom with her hands. She had not intended to mention any of what Reverend Carter or any of them had said, but in the clean kitchen with good summer food on the table and a glass of iced tea in her hand, Zorrie found some of her warmth about church coming back. She had brought over apple pie, and as

she spooned sour cream onto the slices she'd cut, she said she'd
been enjoying the services lately and asked Noah if he'd ever
given any thought to going up to Hillisburg on Sundays.
Noah said he had not. Zorrie looked carefully at him to see
if the question had bothered him, but he gave no outward sign
that it had. After a moment, she asked him why not. Noah
said, very simply, that it wasn't a place for him. That it had
been a comfort and refuge to his mother, and he appreciated
that, but it was not a place he was going to go and pass time,
on Sunday or otherwise.

Aware that she had stepped into areas that weren't necessarily hers to step into, not least just a week after Noah had set
his own barn on fire in hopes of being hauled off to the state
hospital, and less than three days since he had started to settle
down, Zorrie would have left it at that, but Noah seemed
inclined to expound. He noted that Virgil had never thought
much of church, but that he had gone until his last years to
please Ruby. Neither one of them had insisted that Noah go
once he was an adult, so he had stopped. He had observed
holidays and on those occasions had never declined to bow
his head at the right times and had recited lines of scripture
for Ruby her last days, but he lacked the call. He thought there
was plenty out there, and allowed that maybe some of it was
even eternal, but he wasn't sure any of it needed a name and
so many little houses built on its behalf in the countryside out
of wood or stone.

Zorrie turned over what Noah had said for the better part
of the afternoon as she and Lester hauled some of the previous
year's grain up to the elevator, and then as she weeded her
zinnias. What she thought about, primarily, was whether or
not she too had come to lack the call, and if her enthusiasm

for it today had been due more to the weather and her excitement about spending another noon meal with Noah. It was certainly the case that in her early days and years with Harold she had had plenty of feeling, had sensed there was something extra, surely divine, in almost everything she did. She looked back at the many hours of praying she had done in the period after Harold's death with gratitude, fondness even, and she certainly did not feel any regret for all the years, even when her enthusiasm had been cut considerably, that she had attended Sunday services. But as she thought about it in the light of her conversation with Noah, she wasn't sure where, or what, the feeling at the heart of it had been.

Without bringing Noah up, she put some of this to Lester that evening as they were looking over the beans. He said that was more Emma's department than his, but he supposed you either had yourself squared away about it or you didn't. He had never much pondered the heaven or hell aspect, but thought that as a reliable outlet for the deeper sentiments there was much about lifting up your voice and bending your head to recommend.

That evening, after a small supper of tomato soup, celery, and crackers, Zorrie sat with Oats and wondered if the feeling, such as it was, was something that took more easily in the young and the old, and that the average person in the middle had to fly some of her years with just the wings of old habit to keep her from crashing. Looking at it this way, she saw the feeling as something that had grown cool but not cold, that there was a center to it that could get encouraged to life again. This encouragement, it seemed to her, ought though to come directly from upstairs and not from other people, and it bothered her that she had brought it up to Noah, that he might think she was after him about it. Maybe there was some feeling in him somewhere and maybe there wasn't, but it wasn't up to her or anyone else to go poking for it and applying bellows in any place but themselves.

She apologized to him the next day. He said there wasn't anything to apologize for. She insisted. He said that the soul was the most valuable thing about a person, that, as Virgil had said, friends and family made up a symphony of souls, and that was something that should always be treated as precious, though not necessarily discussed. Life, Virgil had said, was a good deal about discouragement and fear, and the soul, which was the true heart of humankind whether you looked at it Christian or otherwise, needed a good deal of comforting some way or other if it was expected to soldier on. Zorrie said that, nevertheless, she wasn't proud to have come to his table like a truck-stop preacher and tried to talk to him about getting to a church he knew better than she did and for many more years.

"I think," said Noah, "that the important thing to me about it this second is you coming every day to this table at all."

Zorrie couldn't sleep that night. She tossed and jumped like a strip of bacon in hot grease and more than once rolled her sheets into a rope. She kept getting up and going down to sit on the porch with Oats, who just snored and acted otherwise unimpressed, even when Zorrie nudged her and asked if she thought Noah had meant anything by what he'd said. Oats paid no more attention a moment later when Zorrie told her it didn't matter anyway because she didn't want to know, that she was the crazy one for letting her thoughts keep moving that way. She stood up and pressed her face against the screen and looked as well as she could into the eyes of a carpenter moth who'd set up shop for the night there. She stood and stared at it, wondering what went on over the long nights in its mind, which was small to her but large to it, until she tapped the screen and realized it was dead.

There was a wind rising. The crickets got tired or disturbed and stopped their scratching. Every now and then a bat winged past. She didn't know if it was just the one or two or several of them. She'd put in a Japanese maple some years before, and she could see it at the border of the service light, bending this way and that. Looking out into the yard from the porch, she thought of Harold and fireflies and felt guilty for a moment. Then she asked herself aloud what exactly she thought there was all these years later to feel guilty for.

Sometime after midnight the storm that had been threatening since that afternoon broke hard, and lightning flashed out over the fields. Zorrie knew it was silly, and maybe even inappropriate, but when the thunder smashed its way down through the dark wet air, she couldn't help feeling it had something to do with what she had been thinking about. Noah hadn't said Opal's name since the fire. There had been no talk of letters, not one word about whirlwinds. He had told her how much it meant to have her there. He had said that. It was true.

It was still raining the next day at noon. Zorrie sat straight-backed with her elbows on the Summerses' table and pulled up bites of tenderloin that she had taken considerable time and care over but didn't seem to have any flavor worth getting excited about. If she looked as tired as she was, she resembled something Oats had dragged around the yard by the neck, but Noah hadn't made any comment about it. In fact, he made little comment about anything beyond the positive qualities of the meal and the poor state of the weather and certainly did not repeat what he had said about being glad she was with him. Not that she had expected him to. Later in the night she had told herself that she had probably just heard the first and last such pronouncement Noah was likely to make, and that he had almost certainly not meant it the way she had taken it. Still. Hank had seen it. Had been seeing it for a good long while now. It was her he'd called on to help keep watch. Not Candy Wilson. Not Lester. Not any of the others who would have done it if he'd asked, though more or less grudgingly. Hank had seen that gaze of hers going down the lane. Maybe he'd spotted some coming back her way too. She looked at Noah over her crossed silverware and off to the side of her glass and to the left of the blue paper napkin she held half crumpled in her hand, and she couldn't get herself to believe that there wasn't ever going to be any chance. Somehow, and she knew there was an improbable alchemy at work even as she sat there picking at her tenderloin, this got translated into there was some chance, and then, later that afternoon, after she had gotten home and was tugging half-heartedly at the scrub-weed crowding out her carrots, that chance didn't have anything to do with it and she had to act.

Only she didn't know what to do. Over the next few days, she kept getting Noah his dinner and sitting with him, both of them saying very little. Once he had a kind of relapse that took him in the middle of the hamburgers over to the window to stare at the wreck of the barn. As he stood there, shaking his head and muttering, she imagined trying out some of the phrasings she'd come up with in her bed or out on the front porch or standing in line to pay for meat in town. She had made whole speeches in her head about how love had come to her in a late-night vision as a blanket made of whispered words that would keep you warm forever, like radium had been supposed to. The promise of love and whispered words was true, while radium was false, she had said to herself, and she had felt it deeply, but there at Noah's table the idea of saying such things aloud left her feeling aghast, like she would either burst out laughing hysterically or start to cry. When Noah sat back down and excused himself for getting agitated again, she felt a little like—though she had said nothing at all—she'd already played her hand and learned it was a bad one, that she should have just folded, and she couldn't speak at all. Sitting there, she saw herself as a kind of charlatan, a scheming opportunist who had seen an advantage in a situation that a decent person wouldn't take. Never mind if—as Zorrie had put it to herself—Noah's act had been one of desperation, a kind of last gasp meant to exorcise the whispers of a feeling grown too tenuous to maintain. Blueberry-eyed Opal had once sat at this table, and she was still out there with her caves and dirt mounds, an hour's drive away, perhaps spinning records if the player Zorrie herself gave her had held up, or sitting down to a lunch of her own.

She thought these things, but looking at Noah, whose own eyes were calming, turning gentle and a little distant again— this man who, she had begun allowing herself to think openly, she had at least halfway loved since she had seen him standing beside a bonfire all those years before—she set objections aside and went back to running through the simpler part of her prepared phrasings. "Noah Summers, Noah dear, Noah darling . . ." When Noah cleared his throat and remarked that it looked like the sun was going to come out, she smiled, opened her mouth, slammed it back shut, nodded, and smiled again.

The sun did come out. The forecast called for yet another storm, but for a few hours the clouds dissipated or took themselves elsewhere, and the sky looked in the interval like a child's bright rendering of summer, with numerous small birds singing across it and a huge, warm sun. Zorrie squinted up as she walked home and thought that this sky and clear light must mean something, or ought to if it didn't. Though they hadn't spoken in some while, she picked up the phone and called Marie in Ottawa, but there was no answer. She turned quiet loops around the front porch and kitchen for a time, wondering if Marie's failure to pick up the phone in turn might be a sign. She wondered if she ought to dig out Virgil's old Montaigne, see if she could find any augury in it, or maybe see if she could remember an odd or an even number of world capitals, which might tell her something, then abruptly decided she had grown tired of herself, bone-weary of her mooning and hesitations. She was a fifty-six-year-old widow and making herself sick, and it had all gone on too long. At a loss, she bent her head and said a prayer to ask for guidance. Then she said another, more loudly this time, about her need to know what was going to be what one way or another. That it was time now. She stood still a moment with her fists clenched and eyes closed to see if she would hear or feel something that might be an answer. The house was quiet and a little warm. Somewhere out in the yard a woodpecker started knocking after grubs, and a minute later a truck went by. "I don't know what that means," she said aloud to the boxes of CoCo Wheats and Saltines she opened her eyes to. She went outside, sat down on the back steps, wrapped her arms around her knees, called Oats over to her, and did not move for the better part of an hour. Then she went upstairs, pulled out a light blue cotton dress, and put it on.

Noah wasn't in the house. She checked in the garden and found only a small rabbit, sweat bees, and a busy swirl of blue and yellow butterflies. Not sure where he might be, she went out to the edge of the field where, before he had set his barn on fire, he had carefully lined up his Cub tractor, push mower, rototiller, and wagon. She couldn't see over the corn, so she climbed up onto the tractor and stood there awkwardly with her hand over her eyes. Off in the distance over at Duff's, someone was towing a load of hay or straw. What looked like it might be a hawk was holding its position in the air over the gravel pit, and big heavy clouds were gathering to the south around Indianapolis. She stood there for quite some time, not really looking, just waiting. Then she heard hammering out by the old corn crib where Ruby had kept her pots and garden tools and climbed down. "All right," she said to herself as she brushed off and straightened her dress. She went and stood with her arms folded under the gnarled branches of a crab-apple tree she knew Noah would have to walk by if he came back to the house when he was done.

WELL BEFORE DAWN, when the fresh storm had settled into heavy rain, she pulled the truck out and drove it past the dark Summers house, east along 28 as far as the Kempton turnoff, then north through town, where the rain beat off the roofs of cars, deepened puddles on the asphalt, and fell in thick streams past the ornamental trees and porch lights with their fancy globes. She kept heading north for a time, skirted a cemetery she'd always thought was pretty and had always meant to stop in and visit, then rode along flat houseless roads that had only the beans and corn and occasional summer wheat growing up along their borders to distinguish them. She drove fast at first, leaning up over the steering wheel, her tires skidding and crunching the wet gravel, but after a while she felt foolish and more conspicuous than she liked, even if it was still so early, and she eased off. Her thought had been to ride around in the dark and rain near home until she could wake up and think straight or at least start to think, but she had run through Forest, past Gus and Bessie's house and the church that had long since stopped having any particular meaning besides pale memories for her, looking gray and lonely in the drenched half-light, and still her mind wasn't offering her anything like help. So after a while she dropped down onto Division Road and took it east, then headed up over around Rossville, past the corner where Mr. Thomas's schoolhouse had stood until someone had knocked it down for its brick and chimney stone, and along a stretch of road that had once led to her aunt's house and now led nowhere in particular because it too had been knocked down, its foundation dug up and soybeans planted over it. As she drove, she held her teeth clenched tight, and held them clenched long after she'd registered that doing so was not accomplishing anything at all.

The sun was up as she rolled by the now barely recognizable outposts of her childhood, but the air was so full of water and the clouds so thick that she might as well be driving through a grotto, barely lit and far below the surface of some distant sea. She kept driving east, heading in the approximate direction of Lafayette, then began taking every turn she came to. Once she passed a bleary-eyed farmer sitting at the end of his driveway in a Dodge pickup, but apart from that, she saw no one. She drove and drove, and when she realized she was lost, even right there in the middle of a county she had lived in for just about every scrap of her life, she pulled off down a lane, cut the lights and engine, and got out. She put on her hat and walked the length of a short field of spindly-looking beans she would have been embarrassed to claim, past chest-high, mud-spattered corn that didn't look much better. She kept walking, teeth clenched again, breathing through her nose, trying to think and not being able to get beyond the condition of the corn, the color of the sky, the character of the cold rain. She stumbled and put her hand on wet, rusty barbed wire. Shivering, rain spattering the back of her sun-browned hand as she held it on the length of jagged wire, leaning over, teeth grinding, the long years all fisted up inside her, she looked at the veins on her wrist and had her thought: bloody and clear. But she took deep breaths and rejected it and pulled her hand away.

Shivering now, suddenly tired or awake enough to recognize that she was chilled, she stuck her foot ankle-high in the edge of a small lake that was forming in the high grass, squeezed at her soaked blue dress, and wondered what good it had done her and was doing her now besides acting as a sponge. This image, that she was dressed in a big blue sponge and tromping around in the rain, helped ease her teeth apart and set a hint of curl to her lips. She thought of the turquoise roadster skidding and swerving for her on the road back from Ottawa, then of Janie riding the L of her dreams, and then of the ridiculous speech she had thought of making to Noah under the crab-apple tree but had only said a few awkward words of, and the curl grew into a smile that exploded straight into a sob. Look at you carrying on, Ghost Girl, she thought, wiping at the mess of rain and hair and tears that her face had become. She stepped backward into pure high-water-content Indiana mud and then gave up, crossed her arms over her chest again, threw her head back, and felt it all come down.

VI

and soft green passages and blurry lemon highlights

Later it seemed like a mist had fallen in front of her eyes, and when it cleared, whole herds of years had again gone galloping by. This troubled her more than it had in the past, this coming wide awake to the evidence of time's ruthless determination: this figure thrown back to her from the mirror, with its splotches and thick ankles and twisted fingers and thin gray hair. For the first time she registered that she had started to move gingerly, was creeping almost, that her balance had gone somewhat haywire, that she sometimes even dreaded the morning and the tasks that lay ahead.

In an attempt to compensate, she redoubled her efforts in the field, waking earlier than she ever had and heading for supper only when the birds slowed their singing. Still, she was well aware that throwing long hours at the problem didn't keep her from inadvertently knocking down more corn stalks than she should have or feeling the strain when she lifted something as inconsequential as a half bale of straw. So when she cracked a bone in her forearm falling backward off the corn bin, she wasn't terribly surprised that Evan Newton, her new hired hand, asked Lester to drive over and speak to her about slowing down. Lester, who had been pulled permanently off his own tractor by a bad back and arthritis, cleared his throat, shoved his hands in his pockets, and reminded her that he was eight and a half years younger than she was but still old enough to know all too well that bodies that had spent most of their lives out in the field wore out.

"It's time, Zorrie," he said.

"Time for what?"

"Time for you to ease off a little."

"You mean time for me to sit in at the television and work crosswords or play Bingo with the other old carapaces at church."

"I didn't say that."

"But you might as well have," she said, rapping a knuckle on her cast and, making a show for Lester's benefit of how hard it was, sitting down.

She hired Evan's brother Blake and bought herself a six-speed John Deere riding mower and a pair of what Kmart referred to as "summer yard gowns." In one of these things, which was more or less a double-length pillowcase with the appropriate holes cut out of it and gloried up with about a dime's worth of lace, Zorrie oversaw her reduced field of operations, whacked her sickle at horseweed and anything else coming up where it wasn't supposed to, and, as soon as she got her arm out of its cast, rode her mower around.

For some years she had looked with more than moderate disdain upon her neighbors who sat crook-backed and flop-armed astride the extra-padded yellow plastic seats a John Deere came equipped with and droned back and forth and around for hours, just so at church or at the bank or anywhere they saw each other they could have the upper hand in conversations about their lawns. Many times Zorrie, who for years had thought lawn work should always stand about tenth on the list, had been treated to commentary and insinuations about the objectionable state of her yard, which had resulted in her getting out her old push mower even less frequently. Now, though, as she rode around on her new machine, with its easily adjustable mechanisms, its various well-thought-out safety features, and, yes, its more than comfortable seat, she had to admit that she had, as Candy Wilson gleefully observed, "caught the bug." So much so that when she discovered that even in first gear she could cover all the currently mowable space in a day and a half, she turned the woods between her property and Noah's into what Blake said would look just like a park if she plopped a couple of benches in it.

The expansion of her lawn got her thinking about her garden, which was in a sorry state. Her last push in the fields, not to mention her arm, had resulted in its transformation into a pitiable thing that probably wasn't much interest even to the groundhogs. The last time a garden she was involved with had looked this bad was when she was a newlywed and had taken it over from Harold. Even then she didn't think there had been quite this many weeds. So she pulled and dug and salvaged and stretched string and replanted and watered and by early August had a dirt pantry worth talking about. There were corn and peas to freeze and beans to be canned. On a whim she'd put in jalapeño peppers and found she enjoyed the taste of them cooked and sprinkled generously over a slice of frozen pizza or in a toasted cheese sandwich, though when she offered this delicacy up to Evan and Blake they just looked at each other, then at the sandwiches, then mumbled something about getting back to work.

Lester called one evening in late August and said he and Emma were going down to the state fair the next day and wondered if Zorrie would like to come along. It had been years since she'd been to the fair, and at first she was put off by how much it had grown. For one thing, you had to park about a mile from the entrance, so that all you saw as you walked up were cars parked in endless dusty rows. Then there were the crowds. There had always been a lot of activity at the fair, but either there were more people in attendance or there were more displays and rides and food stalls packed into the same space. Lester said he thought it was probably both. Emma suggested they go over and see the pigs, that last year it had been quieter there.

The hog barn was not only quieter but somewhat cooler, and Zorrie started to relax as soon as they'd walked in. The big sows and boars lay asleep in piles of sawdust or snuffled at their food buckets or looked dreamily out at them with their intelligent eyes. In one empty stall, a group of small girls was sitting at a card table playing Go Fish, with a pair of drowsy grandparents looking on. There were children everywhere, most of them in shiny boots and sharp Wranglers, tapping confidently at their animals with prods. The show ring was at the far end of the barn, but the sound of the announcer carried easily over the crowd. Occasionally they could hear scattered applause. Aerosol spray cans were in use to keep smells down.

Zorrie said she wished she hadn't given up keeping stock, but Lester felt she'd let go of a fair amount of trouble when she did. Zorrie, thinking of Mrs. Thomas, said it hadn't been all that bad, that there'd been some good company that had come along with it. Lester inhaled and said he wasn't sure if good was necessarily the word, then added that if it was a question of company, she'd do as well or better to get herself another dog. This comment was made lightly, and Zorrie knew Lester hadn't thought before he said it and shouldn't have had to, but she went quiet for a minute just the same. Oats had died a very old, sweet, toothless dog more years before than she cared to count, but Zorrie still missed her terribly. Every now and then, when she wasn't thinking, and sometimes when she was, she clicked her tongue and called out Oats's name.

They ate deep-fried steak sandwiches and deep-fried Bermuda onions and deep-fried green tomatoes and deep-fried elephant ears at a picnic table that had a view of the rotating lights of the carnival rides. Lester said they ought to lower themselves down into the deep fryer and be done with it, and Emma said she felt certain she was about to start perspiring corn oil, both of which remarks made Zorrie laugh. She struck up a conversation with a couple from Jasper who were at the fair as part of a church group, though where the rest of their group was they didn't know. The couple were very large with small, friendly faces and had huge plates of beef barbecue sitting in front of them. They raised flowers out of a row of greenhouses on the back of their property and had taken advantage of the church trip to the fair to celebrate their tenth year in business. They didn't say very much more about it, beyond a few comments about bulbs and tulips, but listening to them, Zorrie got an idea she chewed on the rest of the day and all the way home. She thought about it as she sat, exhausted, eating a celery stick in her chair in the living room that night, and again the next morning before she went out to water. After breakfast, before getting started on the windows put off from the day before, she took out her atlas and started flipping through the pages.

At lunch she looked at an old copy of *National Geographic* that had an article on the tulip industry of Holland. She spent a long time peering at the rows of orange and yellow and pink and red tulips and at the windmills and canals and people on bicycles and beaches along the seacoast. She read the article that accompanied the pictures carefully. There was a mention in it of clouds gathering over rough waters. That evening she opened her old cigar box and, without touching the tin of Luna powder, pulled out her packet of letters from Harold. She had tied them up with string so many years before that she couldn't remember having done it. Among them was the announcement she had received of Harold's death. She read it through twice, then opened her atlas again and traced a line with her finger down from Amsterdam to The Hague and out into the waters of the channel beyond.

She bought a suitcase, applied for a passport, signed on with a tour, and left Halloween Day. Blake took her to the airport and stood smiling in his dark blue Pioneer Hybrids hat at the gate as she walked down the tunnel and onto the plane. A stewardess greeted her with a bright "Happy Halloween" and pointed her to a seat next to a man who, despite the pressed suit he was wearing, looked like he ought to be out on a football field. As she got settled, a small boy walked by, wearing a black cape and plastic vampire fangs.

EVEN THOUGH SHE changed planes three times in three places she had never been, it seemed like she never really quite left her seat, that the next twenty-three hours were spent in the dim light one row in front of the smokers, next to large men or women in jogging suits or fidgeting children, far from the windows and their views out onto dark or light nothing. She wondered if Harold had ever gotten his plane this high, or at least high enough so that down to him had seemed, like it did to her in that shuddering fuselage, as distant as up. But sitting there, riding through what the deep voices of the pilots referred to as pockets of turbulence, some of which elicited gasps from her fellow voyagers, Zorrie was pleased to discover that the prospect of falling from the sky did not bother her as she had feared it might. If something happened, it would all be over and that would be that. She slept soundly almost all the way from New York to Amsterdam.

So strange did the following days seem to her that she barely registered the other members of the small group she was part of. It was rainy and cool and everything in the city seemed to glitter. They rode a boat on the canals, ate fried potatoes with mayonnaise, and went to the Mauritshuis museum in The Hague, where Zorrie stood for a long time in front of a little painting of a goldfinch tied to a perch and another of the city of Delft, with its buildings reflected in silvery water. She had seen her share of paintings before, but these seemed of a different order, works birthed into the world by another process entirely, one that must have involved much patience and many years. She was surprised, because she had not done it in so long, to find herself humming as she stood there looking at the chained bird and at a pair of tiny women talking together in dark dresses as Delft rose across the river beyond, and after a minute realized it was "Love Me Tender," which had been playing on the canal boat.

She had slept so little the night before that she almost didn't go along for the visit to the house of Anne Frank, then found herself so transfixed by the narrow stairways and low ceilings and photographs of Anne and her family that when the group had free time on their last day in Amsterdam, she stood in the long line and climbed up to the secret annex again. On the bus ride down to the American Cemetery at Margraten she read the copy of Anne's diary that she had purchased in the gift shop, and even as she followed along with the group on their tour of the fields of white crosses, she found herself thinking not of Harold, who had left nothing behind to be buried except in a cigar box that had stopped glowing years ago, but of the young girl, soon to die in unspeakable circumstances, who had written, "Think of all the beauty still left around you and be happy."

The final day, the group went to Scheveningen by the sea, and while most of her fellows were content to sit over Dutch waffle cookies and cups of hot coffee and write postcards and watch the rain, Zorrie went out onto the beach and down to the water and did not mind one bit that she had no umbrella or that her good shoes got quickly soaked. This time she did think of Harold, for if some small part of him lay under a sprinkling of worn-out Luna powder, not to mention in the treacherous folds of her heart, the rest of him was somewhere out in the deeps before her.

Although she had stood that time probably no farther than a hundred yards from mist-shrouded Lake Michigan, she had never seen anything larger than a good-sized pond before, and she had certainly never seen waves. Over and over again they rushed up the wet sand toward her, only to pull away again. Everything smelled of salt and depth. There were shells and gleaming curls of seaweed at her feet and gulls over her head. A boat with an orange sail gusted off along the horizon. She tried to follow it all with her eyes and found it brought to mind a windy day and a field of young green wheat, but the white-capped green waters before her never stopped moving, or roaring, so the comparison couldn't hold. What she had before her was unlike anything but itself. And it struck her that if this marvelous surface was what Harold had fallen through and disappeared under, it wasn't all bad. The fires that had ripped him out of the sky would have been instantly doused and the plane cooled. Harold and his fellows would have ridden down to their rest through bubbles and currents and cold, soothing water into a world of quiet wonder.

"Full fathom five, thy Harold lies," Zorrie said aloud. "Of his bones are coral made; those are pearls that were his eyes." The words had come to her, across the ocean and over the ponds and lakes of time, from Mr. Thomas's classroom. She couldn't remember what followed, only the ending, and standing there in her wet, sandy shoes, she realized that the watery strangeness before her spread unimpeded from channel to sea to oceans bigger than any atlas could indicate or any conversation cover. It made the earth and the air that enveloped it seem bigger, for it was made of eternity, and eternity was what held all things, including her. She had imagined that at some point during the trip she might cry, but if it was just rain and salt spray on her face or tears she couldn't have said.

As she sat later after a hot shower over her own cup of coffee with Anne's diary on the table before her, she tried to imagine whether she would have been brave as the fires grew and the waters rushed up toward her, or as the walls of her hiding place grew smaller and the Germans came nearer, but found she was too tired to pursue it. There was a bouquet of blood-red peonies on the table by the sugar bowl. Lights were coming on, and the darkening sea filled the window beyond. A mirror in a heavy frame hung next to an ornate clock, and a waitress was slowly filling cups with tea. All of it looked like something that could hang on the wall next to the paintings she had admired at the Mauritshuis. When one of the guides came and stood a moment beside her and tried to engage her in conversation, Zorrie just smiled and shook her head.

On the plane out of Amsterdam she sat next to a middle-aged American woman named Ellie Storms. Ellie had soft, tired-looking features and long, complicated hair that she touched at from time to time. She was from Kansas City, Missouri, though she had family near Evansville, Indiana, where she often visited. When Zorrie heard this, some of the feeling she had had, standing on the beach with the wind-hoisted sprays of salt-rich moisture scoring her hands and face, returned to her, and it suddenly seemed more important than anything to talk about home. Sitting in her narrow seat far above and half the wide world away from the corner of

Clinton County where she had taken the majority of her life's breaths, the people who had made up the texture of her days seemed rare, even precious, and she found herself talking about them as if they had all accomplished wondrous things. Snow lilted down out of the skies she evoked, great oaks shook and crashed, hot dogs sizzled deliciously, and bonfires roared. Her time in Ottawa was a part of it. Her work alongside Janie and Marie—who in the end had quietly succumbed to a heart attack the previous autumn, and not to the cancer she had fought so cheerfully for so long—became hushed and lovely. Hank Dunn, long since retired, went whooshing forever down the quiet roads in his patrol car. Everything she spoke of seemed informed by beauty. Death had nothing to do with it. Not even for those who were dead. Life was everything. Ellie nodded and listened. At one point, she reached over and squeezed Zorrie's hand.

Later, when Ellie had shut her eyes and sunk back into her chair, it occurred to Zorrie that even though she had spoken of Evan and Blake, Lester and Emma, Candy Wilson, Harold and a number of his fellow departed, she had not once mentioned Noah. Dear Noah. Closing her own eyes, her head warm from the wine she had taken in her high spirits with the dinner of sorry peas and sorrier chicken, she wondered about this omission, wondered how so much, even things you desperately wanted to hold on to, faded from memory, while other things burned their traces so deeply they never left you. The shame of her rejection and the foolishness and guilt she had felt for having incurred it with her presumption and attempt at a kiss under the crab-apple tree in her blue dress were still very much with her, still made her wince or pull up short from time to time. If only she had stayed home that day.

If only she hadn't worked at her hair and pinched at her cheeks and put that dress on. Noah had been devastatingly kind when she had made it clear why she had come to stand waiting for him with her arms crossed under his crab apple. When she had reached out her hands and placed them for an awkward second on his shoulders while his own remained implacably at his sides. So that although he had then spoken, the emphatic immobility of his arms and hands had already offered up all the answer her petition required. The meals had stopped, as had, though much more slowly, her gazing with longing down the lane. But this hadn't kept Zorrie from continuing to think about Noah over the years that had elapsed since that day, from still holding him gently, so gently, in her mind.

She had been thinking about him, she now realized, when she looked at the narrow buildings along the canals, when the bus whirred along the long, flat roads, when she was standing before the painting of the stoic little finch and the waters of the channel, when she told Ellie about those she had known and loved and lost in her life: Bessie, Gus, Virgil, Ruby, her beloved, long-dead Harold, even her long-dead aunt, whom she had lain beside beneath the Christmas tree, and the parents she had barely known. She thought about Noah ever more alone and retreated from the world, surrounded by his letters and sunk into his own thoughts in the shed he had built around the ruins of the barn, around that bit of wall with those irreversibly conjoined names on it, and could still feel that pull in her gut, which, even linked as it was now with her shame and guilt, she relished as much as she ever had.

During one of his outbursts at the table, when he had started to resign himself to the fact that they weren't going to come and get him and take him to Opal, Noah had said it didn't matter how infrequently you laid eyes on your loved one, that you could still love her fiercely, that love and distance were not incompatible, were not necessarily "an inverse." He had then quoted a poem or part of a poem that Opal had seen in a book on French poets—left by a visitor to the hospital—and sent him:

My heart is the same as an upside-down flame

The words, Noah said, had been arranged to form a picture of a heart. Zorrie had often thought about that heart since Noah had told her, with her arms crossed back around her blue dress in the wake of her failed attempt that day, that his wife was still alive even if her poor, good husband wasn't, and that maybe she better not come down to the house with his dinner anymore. As she began to doze, she wondered if when you rode in airplanes, love, even old impossible love, sent hearts tumbling end over end.

IN THE WEEKS and months following her trip, things seemed to need to grow quieter in Zorrie's life. The winter was long and extra cold, and she didn't get out much beyond church and trips into town. Once she let Evan convince her to go over to the high school and watch a ball game, but while she cheered with the home crowd whenever their team scored, and did enjoy watching the young bodies run up and down the court with their bright uniforms and orange ball, she found herself completely worn out when she got home and declined to go again. She preferred to spend her evenings in her chair, occasionally turning on her television to watch the news or a movie, or even working a crossword.

One evening while she was debating whether to open up a can of corned beef or just have half an apple for her supper, there was a knock on the door. She pulled it open and found Noah standing there, holding out a small white box. She opened it onto a stained-glass blue jay Noah said she could hang in the window to catch the afternoon light. Then he thanked her for having sent Opal the scarf covered in tulips, which Zorrie had picked out in the gift shop of the Mauritshuis. Opal had written Noah about it and called it the prettiest thing she had ever seen. Noah said he had had a dream or two recently about Zorrie riding out on the ocean, and had wondered how she was getting on.

"Do you want to come in?" she asked.

"No, I don't think I better, Zorrie," Noah said.

She hung the jay in the south window. She liked the bits of blue it threw onto the windowsill and dining room table and how it constituted a handsome counterpart to the glass cardinal she knew hung in Noah's own south window.

In early March, she set up the grow lamp and started seedlings in the basement. As the little green heads pressed their way up through the moist dirt, she felt some of her energy returning. When it was time, she set to work in the garden, but got discouraged when she found the rototiller difficult to handle. Lester told her she was probably still worn out from racing around the world, but she wondered. The crisp spring air seemed colder than it ever had, and the wind more cutting. More than once as she put in her early garden she stopped in the middle of what she was doing and went inside to stand a moment by the stove or one of the radiators. Before long, though, she was back outside and picking up the shovel or hoe.

By late April the garden was in shape: pale green rows coming out of the black dirt behind the irises, daffodils, and tulips she'd brought back as bulbs from her trip. One morning a young tabby turned up and wove her way through the brilliant greens and yellows to rub herself, like so many cats before her, against Zorrie's leg. The cat had a sore eye and a soft, insistent meow. Zorrie reached her hand down and felt the bones sticking up out of her back and the way the small frame shivered as she held her fingers against it. She brought her out some milk and sliced turkey. When she was finished, she took hydrogen peroxide to her eye. The cat seemed exhausted and more or less slept through her treatment. That evening Zorrie propped open the porch door and put water in a bowl, and the next morning she found the cat curled up and snoring on a worn blanket in the corner.

As the days warmed, she felt she had her stride back and spent respectable stretches in the garden or on her mower. She returned to keeping what she called work hours and was usually out and about when Blake or Evan drove by and, though she had begun allowing herself occasional naps, generally still vertical when they left at the end of the day. She did note, however, that when she listened to Blake's reports on the farm, she asked plenty of questions but rarely wished she had been out there.

In June she got a letter from Ellie Storms. Ellie had had a hard time settling back into her life in St. Louis after her time in Europe and found herself, as she contemplated stacks of receipts and documents that needed her attention, wanting to turn her mind to pleasanter things. She wondered how Zorrie was doing now that she was home from her own trip. After a day or two of thinking about it, Zorrie wrote back. At the start of the letter she had just meant to fill Ellie in on her doings, but before she'd gotten much beyond the appearance of the tabby, who was now more than mildly pregnant, her pen took a turn and she started writing about how she'd been tired lately, couldn't hold on to her hoe, was taking rests she wasn't proud of, and just generally wasn't as motivated about getting her work done. She had often thought of Anne Frank, who had stuffed her short life with so much wonder, while here she was, having been granted many more years, just going through the motions like she was a ten-penny wind-up doll. The world, she wrote, felt like it was slipping straight out of her fingers, that its contours and particulars were falling away. She felt like a beach or like the sand dunes she had once gone for a walk on and didn't know what shape she would be in the next time a wave or some wind decided to saunter by. She closed by referring to their talk on the airplane, about how grateful she was that Ellie had listened to her ramblings with such generosity.

Ellie wrote back the next week, and Zorrie read the letter several times. In her neat, sloped hand, Ellie talked about how it seemed right and natural to slow down, that she had studied about it at school and seen the truth of her studies reflected in her own parents and in the world around her. The body was a beautiful mechanism, and part of that beauty lay in its precariousness, its finitude. Ellie thought mortality was a good thing, as it kept the earth and its wheel of wonders in true. She said that she knew it was easy to talk about but quite another to make the acquaintance of its symptoms, and she understood that it was probably hard, especially for someone who had always been so active, someone who had, "in her golden years, thrown open the doors of her world, taken to the skies and let the poetry shine through." Zorrie worried for a long time over what to write back and made several starts. None of them seemed to express much at all, let alone how the letter had made her feel, and she finally fetched Janie's old postcard from its home of many years in Montaigne, glued it carefully to a piece of heavy, folded paper, and before she put it in an envelope with Ellie's address on it, left off any explanations and just wrote, "Thank You."

Later that summer, when lack of energy became shortness of breath and the blur at the edges of her vision began to creep in, Zorrie found herself thinking more frequently of Ellie's letter than just about anything else. She would lie down on the daybed, turn her back to the room, think of throwing the doors open, and look at the white wall. After a time, she was amazed to see that the depths she had sensed by the shores of Lake Michigan and that she had ascribed to the green waters of the sea at Scheveningen were shimmering right there in front of her. Occasionally Harold or Ruby or Virgil or Janie would come and sit on the edge of the bed, put a hand on her back, and say her name. But mostly she would just lie there, very still, turning it all over in her head.

ACKNOWLEDGMENTS

Claudia Clark's *Radium Girls: Women and Industrial Health Reform* and Kate Moore's *The Radium Girls: The Dark Story of America's Shining Women*, as well as Carole Langer's documentary *Radium City*, were all essential to understanding and writing about luminous dial painting and its tragic after-effects. I also kept *A Simple Heart* by Gustave Flaubert, *The Waves* by Virginia Woolf, *The Histories* of Herodotus, *The Essays* of Michel Montaigne, and *The Diary of a Young Girl* by Anne Frank close to me as I wrote.

I was encouraged and supported in this endeavor by many, including but not limited to, the three Hoosiers in the dedication, Eleni Sikelianos, Eva Sikelianos Hunt, Lorna Hunt, Anna Stein, Morgan Oppenheimer, and Liese Mayer. Thank you all.

A NOTE ON THE AUTHOR

LAIRD HUNT is the author of eight novels, a collection of stories, and two book-length translations from the French. He has been a finalist for the PEN/Faulkner Award for Fiction and won the Anisfield-Wolf Award for Fiction, the Grand Prix de Littérature Américaine, and Italy's Bridge Prize. His writing has been published in the *New York Times*, the *Washington Post*, the *Wall Street Journal*, and many others. He teaches in the Literary Arts Program at Brown University.